ACTIONS WITH CONSEQUENCES

ACTIONS WITH CONSEQUENCES

VIRDEZ EVANS

ACTIONS WITH CONSEQUENCES

This is a work of fiction. All of the characters, names, incidents, organizations, and dialogue in this novel are either the products of the author's imagination or are used fictitiously.

iUniverse books may be ordered through booksellers or by contacting:

iUniverse
1663 Liberty Drive
Bloomington, IN 47403
www.iuniverse.com
844-349-9409

Because of the dynamic nature of the Internet, any web addresses or links contained in this book may have changed since publication and may no longer be valid. The views expressed in this work are solely those of the author and do not necessarily reflect the views of the publisher, and the publisher hereby disclaims any responsibility for them.

Any people depicted in stock imagery provided by Getty Images are models, and such images are being used for illustrative purposes only. Certain stock imagery © Getty Images.

ISBN: 978-1-6632-1066-1 (sc)
ISBN: 978-1-6632-1092-0 (e)

Print information available on the last page.

iUniverse rev. date: 01/22/2021

CHAPTER 1

At 2:45 p.m. on a Friday in the city of Warren, Ohio. It's pouring down raining when Vicky walks in the house from doing some shopping, for the home that she shares with her man. Victoria "VIC2CUTE" Jordan, better known as Vicky. She is about 5'7" tall, has brown eyes, has black hair that comes down her back, and brown skinned with an ass and curves to match the perfect 36B breast she has. As she's putting the groceries away her man startles her by walking up behind her, hugging her and giving her a kiss on the cheek.

"What's up bae?" Face says.

"Woooo boy! You scared a bitch I didn't know you were home," she said.

"Yeah I don't gotta be at work til 4:00, I'm bout to take a nap wake me up at 3:00 boo. I see you put some food up in here finally," he says, walkin' to the room.

"Bae cut it out you know yo ass don't ever go without in this house," Vicky says.

Face just laughs as he enters their room. MoneyFace "Face, is 5'9 1/2" tall, muscular build, light brown skin complexion, with tattoos covering his upper body. He has brown eyes, corn rolls braided to the back. The ladies can't resist him, they seem to melt inside from the moment they see him.

As he lays down, he thinks to himself, 'She ain't never lied, she always make sure a nigga straight. Damn I love my God,' as he drifts off, he said, "I gotta do something special with her ... Zzzzzzzzz, zzzzzz." He dreams.

It's November 28, 2010. Face is in the County on the phone arguing wit Vic. "Yo, I'm telling you now don't come up here to get me in the morning I'm cool on you real shit. You gonna wait til a month before I touch down to get on some fuck shit wit a nigga, you ain't been down here in the last month Vicky. But you want a nigga to get out and fuck wit you like everything good wit us," he says into the phone.

"Nigga what I don't give a fuck bout none of that shit you talking. I know bet no bitch be down dere to get you, cause you already know what it is flat-out," said Victoria.

"Look Vicky, I'm just sayin' I feel like we ain't on the same page right now dat's all. And I'm cool, a nigga been stressing bout a lot of shit lately. Wit my cusin Killa passing last month and you just got ghost on me when I needed you the most," he says.

"So you serious bout not wanting me to come pick you up in the morning?"

"Yeah man," he said.

"Nigga fuck you and when I see you I'ma run yo ho ass over," she says.

"Bye Vicky."

"Nah nigga you bet not hung up on me." Click. "Hello, hello." Unn unn unn. 'Don't worry I'ma be right down there bright and early,' she thinks to herself.

Face walks away from the phone and goes to his cell. "Damn I gotta get this money when I touch down. Me and my girl beefin', I got nowhere to stay I damn sure ain't stayin' at her crib," he says to himself, just as Oz walks into the cell. Oz is his homie from the streets.

"Yo what up whore," Oz said.

"Shit bruh, I can't call it trippin' bout wifey," Face says.

"Who Vic? Y'all stay into it man. Why you trippin' for my nigga you bout to be out tomorrow? I only got a few weeks behind you bruh, and you know we bout to get this bread," Oz says.

"True but that's what I'm sayin' I'm bout to be out there hurting and you know a nigga can't live like dat. Den I got, Vic on a nigga's line talkin' bout wherever she see me at she running me over," Face says.

"Swear my nigga she said dat," Oz says. "Yeah bruh. You got problems on yo hands my dude." Dey share a laugh.

"Shit crazy," Face says. "Aye what's up doe, what we bout to put together to eat?"

"Shit you know we gotta do something," Oz said.

"Yo, see if Shawn wanna get in a nacho wit us bruh. I'm bout to wash this bag out and come downstairs bro."

"Aight it's a bet," Oz says.

"Damn dat shit was good bro, Oz you think you like dat. Huh?"

"Fa real, I can open up shop out dere when I touch down wit dis shit. Have all dat shit on deck nacho bowls, fruit bowls, creamer pies, banana puddings, swolls, and all dat lil candy's muthufuckas be making," Oz says.

"Hell yeah," Shawn comments. They all bust out laughing.

"Aye doe Shawn what's good doe cuz?" Face says.

"What's up cuz?" Shawn said.

"How much time you looking at for da gun?"

"Man I really don't know yet, but everybody saying dat shit probably going fed doe," Shawn said.

"Word damn bruh," Face says.

"What the fuck you we ain't never gone never be able to win locked up. Man what was you doing wit that shit anyway in a bookbag?" Oz said.

"Shit man, looking for Reggie and Leon's ho ass," said Shawn.

"Y'all family bruh, dat shit stupid as hell," Face said.

"You already know doe, how this nigga is Face," Oz said.

3

"I'm bout to head up here to my cell, and lay it down try to get this night out the way. I gotta lot of shit to think bout. I'ma holla at y'all in the AM," Face says. It's on they say, and keep talking.

"Yo Face?" Shawn says.

"Yooo!" said Face.

"Stay out dere when you get out tomorrow."

"You know how these streets is bruh, so ain't no telling how shit gone play out," said Face.

"But what you can count on tho is me giving A.D., or yo ma some paper for you fam. One love cuz. One," Shawn says.

CHAPTER 2

"Face, Face ..." the guard speaks into the intercom.

"Yooo!" Face yells from being awaken outta his sleep.

"The C.O.'s here to escort you to booking," the guard says.

"Aight I'll be right out there." Then, as he gets up and looks at himself in the mirror, he says to himself, "Damn. I gotta get out here and make something happen." He washes his face, and brushes his teeth. Takes a piss, then just as he walks out the door of his cell Shawn walks up. They embrace each other. Then Face said, "I left everything in there for you cuz. Aye doe whatever you don't want shoot it to Oz."

"It's a bet," Shawn says.

"Love you fam," Face said.

"You too cuz," says Shawn.

"Keep yo head bruh, and hit me up," Face says.

He heads down the stairs, and Oz walks out his cell, sayin', "Damn whore dey been calling you all morning. You act like you ain't tryna leave this muthafucka."

They embrace, and Face tells him that he left everything up there wit Shawn. "But, whatever he don't want is yours."

"Good looking," Oz said.

"You already know my nigga, hurry up and get to the crib so we can get dis bread bro," Face says.

"It's only a few mo' weeks til a real nigga touch," Oz says.

"Hold it down bruh, I'm out here when you hit da street,"

"Bet," Oz says.

As Face, walks out the pod a few other people says something to him. He tells 'em all to hold they head up. Then goes out the door, and sees that the C.O. that's awaiting him is Heather. A tall nice looking lady he's been rapping wit, tryna make moves wit. "What's good Heather?" Face says.

"What's up Face, you leaving today, huh?" she says.

"Yeah, it's bout time dese 4 months felt like forever."

"What's your plans your been thinking bout, that you could do so you won't come back here?" she asked him.

"Really, I don't know. I got my G.E.D. since I been in here, so I'm thinking I'll get in school and sees where the college life gets me," he says.

They enter the elevator that leads 'em to Booking. When she says, "Well that's a good start."

"I know right. Yo, what's good doe, you been thinking bout what I asked you?" Face says.

She looks at him. Raises her eyebrows and says, "What's dat?"

"Yo number, so I can holla at you out here in the real world," he says.

"Boy I already know you done heard by now that I den messed wit yo Uncle Tino."

"Naw I ain't hear dat one, but damn Unk den had dat?"

"Yeah had," she says, and they walk out the elevator.

They enter Central Booking and an officer takes him in the back to change out.

"How long you think you gonna stay out this time?" says the officer.

"What muthafucka?" Face looks up and says as he tying his shoe.

"You ain't out yet, so watch yo tone," said the officer.

"Man hurry up and get me processed yo. I ain't tryna hear that shit you talking," Face tell 'em.

They walk out the dressing room, and Heather tells Face to come sign his release forms for his property. After he finish signing the papers. He says to Heather, "Yo ma get at me when you see me out here, don't be acting like you scared of a real nigga."

She smiles, and says, "Boy bye. Be safe Face."

"Stay up ma," he says.

As the officer who dress him out, says, "Come on Face."

Another C.O. name Glad, says, "He'll be back."

Face says, "Yeah probably for whippin' another one of you C.O.'s asses like I did yours. And I got away wit it dumb muthafucka. Keep yo badge on next time faggot!"

"O.k. Face," the other officer that's escorting him out says. "Stay out the way out there," he says.

'Yea aight. Bitch ass nigga,' Face thinks to himself, as he exits the building.

CHAPTER 3

"It's cold as a muthafucka," he says, to himself as he surveys the parking lot to see if anyone is out there to pick him up. "Dang man, I shouldn't of trip out on Shorty like dat last night. Fuck yo it's cold as a bitch, and I got this silly ass summer shit on. A fucking white Tee, these dumb fucking Evisu shorts, a fresh pair of white and red AF Ones, and a New Era 5950 fitted hat."

Just when he gives up hope and start to jog towards his aunt's house. He hears somebody screaming his name. He stops looking around, but still doesn't see no one. "Face," the person yells, from across the street. Right as he looks, he notice a woman's figure. But he doesn't make out who she is, because he's unfamiliar wit the white 2004 Buick LeSabre the woman's in.

Just as he heads in her direction he realizes that it's his girl Vicky. He thinks to himself, 'Damn I'm glad she's out here. It's cold as fuck.'

He jogs to the car and hugs Vic. Squeezing her ass and kissing her, before they get in the car. "You thought I wasn't gone be out here?" she asked him, as she's pulling out the parking lot.

"Shit I ain't no what to think. You know, you been on dat fuck shit lately," he says.

"Shit nigga, a bitch been going thru it out there fa real. You wasn't here to help me wit nothing. I had to get us a new crib and all, move that shit basically by myself fa real. And all you wanna do is argue on the phone, and having all dese ho's coming to visit you," she says.

"Bae go to Wiggy's crib, real quick before we go to the house. I gotta holla at Rayn bout something," he says. "And I hear what you sayin' bout everything you been going thru out here. But you fucked me up doe, when you stop having bread on the phone for me to call you. Then on top of that you wasn't worrying bout seeing me fa real. Cause you already knew I would of dismiss them ho's," he says.

"Yeah whatever," said Vicky.

"I'm home now boo, that's all that matter. Right?" Face says.

"Yea."

"Hum, give me a kiss bae," Face says. "Muahhhh I love you baby."

"I love you too," Vicky says.

"No you don't," he says with a smirk on his face.

Vicky turns up the music as Face bobs his head to the beat. "Yo, ma who is this?" he ask.

"My peoples from Cleveland."

"Oh word," he listens to 'em for a few mo' seconds then takes the CD out. And puts in that 'Yo Gotti, Cocaine Series Two.'

"Why you take that out for? That's my song bae," says Vic.

"I don't want to hear that shit. Yo ass probably been kicking it wit one of dem niggas," he says.

She looks at him and says, "Whateva nigga don't start."

He just turns up the music and raps along with the lyrics. "Whippin' soda wit do yola / Let me show you how to make some mo bruh / Da da da da, da da da da /"

9

CHAPTER 4

Vicky pulls up to Wiggy's house and parks in the driveway. They get out and Face really looks at the car for the first time. "Damn bae this shit nice, whose car yo got?" he asked her.

"It's mines I just got it like two weeks ago."

"You did dat I ain't go lie boo," he says.

They knock on the door, then hears somebody ask, "Who is it?"

"It's me Aunt Wiggy," Face says.

"Who?" she says.

"Open da door Wiggy," Vicky yells. "It's cold girl." Wiggy opens the door smiling. "Dang you always playing," Vicky says.

"Shut up and come in girl," Wiggy says.

"Hi Bob," Wiggy screams when she sees her nephew (Bob is what they called my grandpa).

"Hi, Aunt Wiggy," Face says, giving her a hug. "Where the kids at?"

"They're in the back, playing," she says.

"Rayn home?"

"Yeah, he in the living room on that damn game," his aunt said.

Face leaves them two to talk, as he go to holla at Rayn to see what's good wit a few dollars or some work to push. "What's up Unk?" he says as he enter the living room.

"What's up boy, I told Wiggy that was you out dere," Rayn says.

"Yeah you know they just let me out that muthafuckin' hell hole this morning," says Face.

Puff, puff, puff and Rayn starts coughing as he trys to pass Face the blunt, while saying something.

"Nah, I'm good on dat Unk, you know I'm still on papers."

"Oh yeah, dem crackers always tryna keep a tail on a nigga," Rayn says.

"Huh bruh," Face exclaims.

"What's good tho nephew? I know you tryna get right out here."

"You already know dis," Face responds.

"You got some paper?" Unk says.

"Hell nah man, you already know that fucked up ass commissary in the County taxing the fuck outta a nigga," Face said. "I was comin' to see what you working wit for a nigga to make a few bucks off of, or if you had a couple dollars I could get out here and get right wit," he says.

"You know I ain't doing shit but going to work and fucking wit da bud a lil bit," says Rayn.

"Dat's what's up," Face says. "Aye doe Unk you think you can get me hired up dere where you working?" Face ask him.

"Probably so, you'll have to come up there in the AM tomorrow and fill out an app," Rayn says. He pauses the game on PS3, that he's playin'. Then they head upstairs to do business. Rayn pulls his stash out and starts weighing the product. "Here Face grab that baggy and take dis."

Face grabs the bag, putting the bud in it. Asking Rayn, "How much is dis?"

"A zip and a half," Unk says. "You good wit dat right?" asked Rayn.

"Most definitely!" Face responds.

They exit the room and go back down the steps. As Face is putting the product in his pocket. They walk into the dining room. The kids see their favorite cusin for the first time in 4 months. "Hi Face!" they yell and run to give him a hug.

"Hey lil mommas," he says. "Y'all been good?"

"Yeah," they say.

"Well I'm bout to slide when I come back I'll have something for y'all. Okay?"

"Yeah. Aight."

"Aunt Wiggy and Rayn love y'all."

"Aight bro," Rayn says.

"Love you too," Wiggy and the girls say.

"Bye Vicky," Rashionna and Rahlaisha says.

"Bye ya'll be good," Victoria tells 'em. "Aight Wiggy and Rayn," she says as they head out the door.

CHAPTER 5

"Let me drive bae," Face says to Vicky. They get in the car and, as he starting the car he ask Vicky, "Where the new house at?"

"On Hamilton St. The address 1532. You remember where Amp Jones mom stay?" Vic ask her man.

"Yeah bae," Face says.

"Well it's a couple houses from there."

As Face drives to the crib, so he can change his clothes and chill wit his woman. He starts to think, bout where he can get the bud off at. 'Ummmm maybe I can get wit Strong and see what's up wit him after I get away from Vic's ass.'

He turns down the music as he coming down Nevada St. approaching Hamilton. "Make this right bae," Victoria says, "and it's two houses down from Amp's mom's crib on the left."

He pulls in the driveway of a white house wit a matching garage. "Damn bae this shit look straight, even tho I would of preferred to stayed where we was at in the white people's neighborhood by Jamestown Village."

"Be thankful you got a roof over yo head bae," she said.

Leaving him there thinking, 'Like yeah she def right.' Face gets out the car and head inside the house. "Damn boo you must of just moved in here, everything still packed up and all outta order," he says to her as she goes to the back room for something.

"I been staying at Kimberly's since I moved here, cause I ain't wanted be here by myself. You being locked up and everything," she tells him.

"I feel it ma," he tells her feeling ashamed that he left her out there unprotected for so long. Beside leaving his high point "45" caliber at the house when he got locked up. "Yo bae, where's my clothes at so I can take this dumb ass summer shit off?"

"All your stuff is back here in the room bae," she responds.

When Face enters their room, he see his prize bent over going through some papers in a lil plastic tub. He admires her perfect shaped ass for a moment. Before walking up on her and bumpin' his manhood on her behind. She looks up at him with lust in her eyes. The same lust that got him caught in her web a few years ago. "What?" he says.

"Boy you know you bout to start something you ain't gone be able to last 45 seconds in," she says to him.

"Wow, you got jokes today huh?" Face say to her as, he takes his shirt off and sit on their bed.

"I'm sayin' bae, you know this kitty kat on exclusive, just the same way you left it," she tells her man.

"Is that right?" he says. "Well come here and show me what I been missing."

She walks up on him and straddles him. Electricity shoots through their bodies as they kiss one another passionately. Missing the effects that they have on each other. "Daddy I miss you," she says, through a soft moan she let out.

"I been missing you too bae," he tells her ...

CHAPTER 6

An hour and a half later, after they finish their making ups to one another wit exotic hot and sweaty sex. Face steps out the shower and heads back to their room. Vicky's lotioning her body while sayin', "Bae I put your boxers and wife beater on the bed. I'm bout to get your socks after I'm finish lotioning."

"Thanks bae," Face say to her.

"Humm boo you want some of this," she says while holding the bottle of lotion in her hand.

"Yeah, bae put some on my back," he tells her. As she lotions him, her hands travels to his dick. Instantly her hands causes his shaft to erect. "Ahh bae it feels so good to be touched by you," he says.

"Do it," she says as she kneels down in front of him and takes him into her mouth.

"Ooh shit ma ... Damn I missed this shit," he tells her as she looks up while sucking him, looking in his eyes at the same time. Ten minutes pass when he cums. "... Oooohh fuck Victoria. Damn you da best," he said.

"Yeah okay let me find dat you done already," she tells him, as she goes and get a rag for him. He lays back on their bed closing his eyes loving his woman. "Hum," she says, throwing the rag at him. "You can't have your cake and eat it too."

He laughs. "... Oh word you go do a nigga like dat," he says.

"Nigga I shouldn't of suck yo lil ass dick, after all that shit you was talkin' last night," she tells him.

"You got dat bae, but don't act like I didn't just max yo ass out an hour ago," he says. She smiles and walks out the room, leaving him to get dress ... "Yo boo?" he calls to Vicky.

"Huh?" she answers.

"Let me see yo phone real quick," he says.

"Hum."

As he goes to grab the phone, he hands her some of the loud (that's Kush) that he got from his aunt's boyfriend. "Roll this up boo, and let me know what it smoke like," he says.

"Ummm ... I been waiting to smoke. I was just bout to call Kim's ugly ass," Vic says to him.

As she's rolling up, he makes a call to his homie Strong. Ring, ring, ring ... the phone rings three times before Strong picks up. "Yoo?" he says into the phone.

"What's up bruh?" Face says back.

"Who dis?"

"Montana!" Face responds.

"Oh what's up," Strong says.

"I can't call it man just got out a few hours ago."

"Oh word bruh," says Strong.

"Yup, I'm tryna see what's up wit you doe I got dat O.G. on deck," Face tells him.

"Shidd bro swing thru I'm on Kenilworth St. Now right behind the Pit Stop (dat's a gas station on my old block)."

"Aight, but I'ma stop and see moms and grams first doe my nigga," Face says.

"Aight. One." They hung up.

"Here bae," Face says as he hands her the phone back. She's puffin' away on the weed he just gave her. When he notices that the 52 inch flat-screen is missing, the one he brought her for Christmas last year. "Yo where the fuck the flat-screen at?" he says.

"What?" she says.

"You heard me Vicky, stop acting simple."

"Ummm," she says, trying to think how to explain what she did.

"Don't tell me you sold da damn TV," he says.

"Ummm, well I huh ..."

"No you didn't," he says.

"I had to bae, when I stop dancing at the club. Money was getting tight and I had to pay the rent," Vicky says.

"What, why da fuck you ain't say nothin'? I could of got one of my peoples to come thru for us til I got out."

"I don't know, but don't trip bae we gone be good," she tells him.

"Dat shit crazy," he says to her shaking his head. "Aye doe bae, I gotta use the car for a min to see my fam, and go holla at Strong," he tells her.

"Aight, but take me to Kimberly's crib while you do that so I won't be in here bored," she said, grabbing her coat. "You don't wanna hit this blunt?" she ask him.

"Nah, I can't smoke they got me on papers," he says.

"Oh you scared now?" she says laughing ...

"Nah, but a nigga can't win out here doing dumb shit."

CHAPTER 7

"Lock the door bae," Vicky tells, me as she's getting in the car calling Kim's number. When I get in the car she's got them niggas from Cleveland's song playing again. I take it she just repping where she's from, since they're from her home town.

I sit back while she drives and listen to the words of the music. And think to myself, 'Like they aight, but dey not fucking wit my shit doe.'

When we pulled up to Kim's crib, I tell Vicky to let me use her phone til I get one later. I give her a kiss and tell her I love her. "I love you too, and don't be all day," she says to me.

Just when I'm pulling out Kim's parking lot, the phone rings. Ring, ring ... I turn down the music and answer the phone. "Yo, what's up? Who dis?" I say.

"Kim wants some smoke bae come in real quick."

"Aight," I say into the receiver.

I walk in Kim's apartment, her shit is laid out. Nice furniture, end tables to match, an entertainment system, mirrors on the walls, nice television, and a pretty ass kitchen table to top it off.

"Hi bro. You wasn't gone come in and say what's up?" Kim says to me.

"What's good sis? You already know a nigga fuck wit you I was just bout to shoot and see moms real quick dat's all." (Kimberly's, Victoria's cusin. But we share a brother and sister friendship.)

"Dat's what's up bro. Let me see dis loud, dis bitch Vicky talking bout you got that's like dat," she says. "And take yo shoes off nigga, dis dat good carpet."

"Girl cut dat shit out," Vicky tells her. I take my shoes off, sit at the kitchen table and ask her what she wants.

"Just a dub bro, dat shit be having me high all day," she says. I eyeball a dub out for her, tell her good looking. "You know I'ma hit you up bro, you just got out I know you tryna come up," she tells me.

"Fasho," I say putting my shoes on. Vicky walks up to me kisses me, and tells me to be careful. I kissed her back, and said, "I will." Then walked out the door.

When I get in the car, I go thru her CD collection to see if she got some of the type of music I like in here. When I came across one of my old demos I made before I just did my County bid. And a smile comes across my face. "She still got my shit," I say out loud. Then change the CD in the CD player, and pull off.

I come to a red light, as I'm reciting my verse I spit on this song called 'Keep It Hunned' ft. my cusin 'Lil Pimp AKA P.I.' "You let yo mans go down for ya pack that ain't one hunnid / You post to sit out yo time and back to that money /," I say, as I stop for the light.

I look to my left and see this nigga they call Gold Mouth, in his cherry red Benz S550 sitting on 24 inch dub floaters. The windows are tinted on my girl's car, so he can't see me admiring his car. But I can see him looking at her car trying to see who's driving. The light changes and I step on the pedal leaving him, staring at her 30 day tags.

My song 'On My Grind' comes on when the phone rings. "... Hello," I say.

"Hello Vicky, oh who dis Face?" Mrs. Regina says in my ear.

"Yeah dis me. Hi you doing Mrs. Regina?" I say.

"I'm doing aight, when you get home?"

"Today," I tell her.

"Hope you stay out," she tells me.

"I am," I say, to her.

"Where Vicky at?"

19

"She's wit Kimberly," I tell her. (Mrs. Regina is Vicky's mother.)

"Okay I'm bout to call Kim's phone. I was tryna see if she knew where I can get some smoke from," she says.

"Where you at?" I ask her.

"Home."

"Oh I'm right here by yo house, unlock the door," I say.

"Okay bye," she tells me.

"Aight," I say.

I pull up to her house, leave the car running and walk inside. "What's up Michael?" That's Vicky's lil brother.

"What's up Face?" he says, and goes back to playing his game system.

Mrs. Regina waves me in the dining room so Michael doesn't see and hand me a 20 dollar bill. I give her the bud. Give her a hug, and tell her I'ma have Vic call her when I get back wit her.

"Okay, thanks for coming thru," she says.

As I'm leaving I stop and give Michael some dap and tell him to tell Troub I said 'What's up?' (That's their older brother.)

"I'ma tell him," he says.

"Aight," I say walking out the door. "Bye y'all."

"Bye," Michael says.

"Bye Face, be safe," Mrs. Regina tells me.

"I will," I tell her and close the door. When I get back in the car I call my mom's phone to see where she's at.

"Hello," she said.

"Hi mom," I say.

"Boy why you just now calling me?" she tells me. "I know they let yo ass out early this morning."

"Mom, I had to go to the crib and get dress, and get myself together real quick," I say, "But where you at tho?"

"At yo grandmother's house," she says.

"Aight I'm pulling up in a few minutes mom. Love you," I say.

"Love you too," she said, then hangs up.

CHAPTER 8

I get to my gram's house, and before I get out the car I put the bud in the glove compartment. I walk into my gram's crib, and everyone's screaming. "Welcome home ... Hi ... What's up cuz? ... Hey brother ..." and, "What's up nephew?"

I tell everyone 'Hi,' and start giving everyone hugs and dap. It's my sisters Seaniece and Cherelle, my Aunt Erika, my grandma, my mom, my lil cusins KeKe and Doop, and Uncle Rose. "What y'all having a party over here?" I say.

"Nah, they went to church wit me this morning. Now they wanna crowd my behind," my grandmother says.

"Face, what's good cuz?" Doop says to me.

"What it do lil bruh?" I reply.

"Nothin' bro when you get out?" he ask.

"This morning," I say.

"We need you out here Vee stay out da way dis time."

"It's a bet lil bruh," I say.

My sister Seaniece comes down the steps from using the bathroom. "Hi brother," she says, giving me a hug. Telling me she missed me.

"I missed you too ugly," I say to her.

I see my mom, Cherelle, and my Uncle Rose as I walk into the dining room. "What's up bro?" Relle says as I give her, my mom, and Uncle Rose all hugs.

"What's up sis?" I say. "Hey mom, how's things been? I ain't heard from you since I wrote you back like 2 months ago, when they had me in the hole," I say to her.

"You got that money order I sent you, right?" says my mother.

"Yeah got it," I say.

"Enough said, you wasn't talking bout nothin' in the letter away boy."

"You still could of wrote me back, dat shi... I mean stuff helps a person's time fly."

"Watch yo mouth now you know mommy in the kitchen," she tells me.

"My bad," I say.

"Nephew what's up, I smell it where's it at?"

"What's up Unk? I got you when I go to the car," I say.

"Bro, let me get some too," Relle said.

I look at dem and say, "Dat's gone cost y'all. Y'all know a nigga fresh out. And I don't smoke, so yeah run it." Relle looks at me like, 'Bro!' "What?" I say.

"Nigga you petty, but I got you doe."

I walk into the kitchen, and grams tell me to sit down and eat something. She's cooked fried chicken, mac-n-cheese, mashed potatoes, greens, and beets. 'Yuck beets,' I think as she hands me the plate. "Thanks grams," I say to her.

She sits down with me and starts to talk to me about my cusin Brandon's (aka Killa) funeral. Tells me it was nice, that our friends from Tennessee showed up and paid their respects. My cusin Chris aka P.I., took it hard. "He was acting a fool," she says.

I tell her, "Grams I would have too. Fa real I can't believe he's gone. I was just in the 'Bus' (dat's short for Columbus, OH) wit him before I caught the violation charge that night I left your house. I just hope P.I. can keep it together," I say. "How's Aunt Crystol, Tony and Dee Dee?" I ask. 'I gotta call her,' I think to myself.

"They're all fine, but it's just a tragedy," she said.

"Yo grams, I'm bout to get up outta here, thanks for the plate," I say.

"How that girl of yours doing? Tell her I said why haven't she been to see me in a while."

"Her straight just moved to Hamilton St. by Oak St.," I say.

"Humm take her this plate, and tell her I said make sure I get my plate back too," she says.

While she makes the plate I go to tell everybody I'm out. They all said they love me and to be careful. My moms gives me a hug and kiss, on the cheek. I do the same and go in the kitchen get the plate from grams. Tell her I loved her and give her a hug and kiss on the cheek. "Be safe out there baby boy," she says to me.

I reach the car and my uncle, and sisters come to the car. Uncle Rose spins forty bucks wit me, and then my sister gives me fifteen dollars, I give her a ti ti (that's half an eighty). I tell her to smoke wit Niecy. Then I beep the horn and pull out. Beep... Beep ... "Keep yo eyes open for these haters bro, love you," my sisters yell to me.

While I'm driving, I'm thinking bout my bruh Killa. And put the song 'Dolla Signs' ft. Ray & Dontae on. Them my niggas I fuck wit. "Face what you doin' I been getting money / Laughing at these broke niggas cause they so damn funny /." I'm turning on Kenilworth St., and see some young niggas hugging my old block. I slide pass dem looking to see if I know any of them. But none of them looks familiar except for one. He got a hoodie on tho, making a transaction wit a junkie, so I really don't get a good look at his face.

"Yooo," one of the youngsters yells at my car and throws his hands up. He looks to be no older than seventeen years old. I stop the car and rolled the window down a lil bit. He runs up to the car. "Yooo, what's up you good?" he ask me.

"What's up?" I say.

"Oh my bad bruh, I thought you might been a Bop," he says.

"Nah nigga I don't fuck around, but I got that smoke doe bruh."

"Oh yeah," he says, "Pull in let me see something for forty."

"Get in," I tell him, when I pull in the parking lot of the store across from Pit Stop. "What's yo name bruh?" I ask 'em.

"Junie," he tells me, as he gives me the money.

"I'm Face bruh," I tell him as I look in his eyes to see if I detect any weakness in him. When I don't I instantly sense I lil respect for him. I hit him off wit the smoke, and tell him to get at me and be safe out here playing the block like dis.

He says, "Aight," then hops out.

I call Strong's number as I pulled out the parking lot of the store. Ring, ring ... "Yo bruh, what house is it?" I say.

"You gon see the white Chrysler in the driveway," he tells me.

"Aight," I say and hung up.

I park in his driveway, grab the rest of the smoke out the glove compartment then lock the door to the car.

CHAPTER 9

I knock on the door to Strong's house. "Who is it?" he says.

"Face," I say.

"What's good? I ain't know you was that close," he says as he's opening the door.

"What's poppin'?" I say, as I step inside. "I was just at the convenience store when I called." We exchange a manly handshake, then go to the back room where he's packing some work up.

When we enter to the room, it's some ho's chilling smoking, they speak. "Hey Face, when you get out?"

"Today," I said to 'em. "What's up wit y'all doe?" I say.

"Shit over here fucking wit Strong's lame ass," the one wit the red shirt, demi blue jeans, and red and grey Tims says. The other one, is just sitting there chinky eyed looking high out the ass. She has sexy long hair looking like she's mixed wit something, her complexion is a flawless light skin with no marks or bruises. She has on a white shirt that hugs her breast, some black leggings, and some white, black, and gray Ken Griffey Jr.'s with a lil pink in them.

Strong, sees me looking at her, and nods his head. Like yeah she bad. I look back at him like yeah bruh. "What's good tho, Strong?" I say. "You fucking wit that raw now?"

"Yeah," he says. "Dis where it's at bruh."

"Dat's what's up," I said. Then I toss him the smoke. "Check this out," I say to him.

Sniff, sniff ... He smells the green. "This shit loud as fuck, how much is this?" he ask.

"A lil bit over an ounce," I say.

He gets up and goes to get the door, ... Knock, knock, knock. He comes back in toss me the smoke, and grab ten packs off the table. Then walks back in the kitchen. Saying, "Weigh dat Face."

I'm weighing it up when I see Shorty wit the Griffey's on whisper something to her homegirl. I look at her, as I hear her say, "Damn girl he fine."

Shorty in the red, says, "Um hmm." I act like I don't hear 'em, and look down at the scale shaking my head. "What you shaking yo head for?" the one in the red shirt said.

As her friend gets up to use the restroom. "At y'all two," I say, when Shorty walk pass me with an ass as fat as, Young Money's rap artist Nikki Minja. "Damn," I said, tryna focus on what I'm doing but still managed to spill a bud or two on the floor.

Shorty in the red, laughs at me. "Ha ha ha ..." she laughs.

Her friend turns around at the restroom door and speaks to me for the first time. And says, "Yea this all me back here too nigga!"

"Shidd, I see it's definitely something serious," I tell her. She just shuts the door, smiling knowing she's fucked my whole head up.

"Yo, what it come out to?" Strong says, when he enters back in da room. He sits the money on the table he just got from his fein.

"It's one zip and like nine grams," I say. "Just shoot me four hundred dollars for it bro."

"Aight," he says, as he goes in he pocket and pulls out a knot of cash handing me the four hundred dollars as Shorty's coming back in the room.

"Good looking," I tell him.

"It's nothing," he says. "Roll some of this shit up," he tell the one in the red.

"Nigga, with what my looks?" she says.

"The blunts on the counter in the kitchen," Strong tells her.

When she gets up I can see she's not too bad herself. Standing bout 5'2" with a body like 'Amazing 100' out of 'The Straight Stunnin' Magazine.' Then it strikes me where I know her from. She use to be wit these girls that use to cum thru the hood. They whole clique was like dat, 'meaning some bad bitches.'

"What's yo name Lisa, right?" I ask her, when she comes back in the room.

"Nigga don't act like you don't know me," she says.

"Nah, it just took me a min to remember yo face," I say. "And what about you?" I ask the other one wit the Griffey's on.

"Terria," she replies.

"Dat's what's up, I like dat," I say.

"It's hard not to when it comes wit a bad bitch like me," she says.

I laugh her comment off. And think to myself, 'Yea I'ma holla at her bout dat, but right now I gotta get this bread.' "Yea aight shawty," I say to her.

"Un uh, cut all dat shawty shit out. I heard that shit all the time where I'm from," she says to me.

"Where you from?" I ask her.

"ATL," she says.

"Dat's what's good, well you in Warren now ma so keep that shit in check round here. Cause I'ma definitely be checking for you when I get my paper right," I say to her.

'Fuck this nigga's fine, he can get it right now,' she thinks to herself. But instead she tells me, "Take yo time boo I'll be around."

"Yeah aight," I say. "Yo Strong, let me holla at you real quick bruh!"

"What's up bruh?" he says, as him and I, step into the kitchen.

"Yo what you get dat food for?" I said to him. (That's herion.)

"Shidd for like one hundred thirty dollars a gee," he says. Knock, knock, knock ... "Who dat?" Strong says, to the person knocking on the back door.

"It's me Tammy." (She's a known junkie from da hood.)

He opens the door. "What's up Tammy, why ain't you call first?" he says.

"My bad Cee ('Cee' is short for Cee-Strong), but can you help me out I'm sick, I'm cramping man bad. I haven't gotten high all day I need you Cee," she tells him.

"Hold up," he says, leaves, then come back wit two packs for her. "Call me first next time or you ain't getting nothing," he tells her.

"I got you baby thanks, and I'll call you wit some money next time too," she said leaving out the door.

"Tammy looks bad man," I said. "She didn't even notice me standing right here," I say.

"Yeah man, I know she fell way off from back in the day," he says.

"Hell yeah," I tell him. "But aye doe, my nigga you said one hundred thirty bones, well I can probably get it better and cheaper. Let me put some shit together and I'ma hit you up and let you know something," I tell him.

"I'm wit it bruh, bruh," he says to me.

"Aight, well look bruh I'ma shoot up here to one of these stores, and get me a phone. That's wifey's number I called you from earlier."

"It's a bet," he says.

"Aight bet," I say. I step back in the back room and tell, Lisa and Terria bye.

Lisa says, "Bye nigga."

And Teria says, "Bye Face."

"It's on shawty," I say, then head to the door.

When I get to the car Vic's phone rings ... "Hello," I say.

"Where you at bae?" I hear Vicky say.

"Just pulled out of Strong's driveway bout to grab me a phone from Exclusive." (That's a store.)

"Oh, okay well when you coming back, cause I wanna see you?" she ask.

"I'm on my way," I tell her, "But then you gon have to take me back to get my phone doe bae."

"Just get yo phone then come get me when you done," she says.

"Okay," I say.

"Aight, love you bae ..." she says.

"Love you too."

CHAPTER 10

I just got my Android LG3 phone, I'm riding down Route 422 better known as Youngstown Rd. Heading back to Kim's crib to get Vicky. As I'm bout to pass my old block I see my homie Five, standing on the block talking to someone in a Tahoe truck. The young kid Junie's still out there too.

I pull in and Five's tryna look in the car to see who it is, I roll down the window and speak. "What's good nigga?" I say.

"Oh shit! What's up lord?" he says.

"All is well bruh," I say. I step out the car to embrace them. And I see it's my cusin A.D. that's driving the Tahoe. He gets out and embrace me as well. "What's up cuz?"

"What's good bruh?" I say.

"When you get out?" they ask.

"This morning," I reply.

"You straight cuz?" A.D. ask me.

"Hell naw man shit bad for a nigga."

"Here take this bro," he says. And hands me two hundred fifty dollars.

"Dat's what's up fam," I say.

"Stay out da way," he tells me.

"Aight, big bruh. I'ma be shooting you or ya moms some bread for Shawn when I get right cuz," I tell him.

"Aight cuz," he says, getting back in the truck.

"Aye, cuz give him my number when he calls you," I say.

"What's the number?"

"(330) 984-5680."

"Aight bro, I'm make sure he get it," he says, then pulls off.

"What's poppin' lord?" I ask Five.

"Nothing man, just out here tryna get it up bruh."

"Dat's a bet," I say. "Yo who dat lil nigga out here?" I say.

"Dat's da homie, he just moved down here from da 'Chi' ('Chi' is short for Chicago)," he says. "He good peoples," he says.

"He vicelord?" I ask Five.

"Nah joe," Five says.

"Yo lil bruh?" I say to Junie.

"What's good Face?" he responds.

"What part of Chicago you from?"

"I'm from da West Side in 'K-Town,'" he says.

"I was just out dere in '09, wit da homie Menace. You hear of somebody name Rusty, he got a B.M. in K-Town?" I ask him.

"Nah, but I heard of the dude Menace," he says.

"Yeah, dat fool ain't nothing to play wit," I tell him.

"He the one who caught that case for dat shit wit dat nigga from da West Side, right?" he ask.

"Something like dat," I say.

"Yo 5 whose whip you in?" Five ask.

"Dis wifey's whip," I tell 'em.

"You ain't got yo shit no more?" he says to me.

"Yea dat shit at pop's crib doe, but I gotta get dese bands up before I go get dat doe bruh."

"Dat's what's up," he says.

"You got some more of dat smoke?" Junie ask.

"Hell nah bruh, dat shit boom like a muthafucka doe," I say.

"I'm bout to go in here and get me a Black-n-Mild real quick," Five says.

"Shidd, bro, here grab me a pack," I tell 'em. Handing him a twenty dollar bill.

"Yo, what's yo number?" Junie ask me.

"(330) 984-5680," I say. "I'ma have some more of dat loud for you later too, bruh. Just call me."

"I got you," he says. Then walks away to catch a play.

Five comes out the store. "Here bro," he says. Handing me the Milds and change back. We chop it up, a few more mins I give my number tell him to call later. Then hop in Vic's car, and pull out to go get my boo.

"Where the hell is this nigga at?" Vicky says, out loud but really to herself.

"You know Face probably out dere flexing in yo shit like it's his," Kim says.

"Girl, let me see yo phone," Vicky tells Kim.

"Here you go," Kim gives her the phone.

Ring, ring, ring ... "Yo what's up?"

"Where the hell you at nigga?" Vicky says.

"I'm turning in the apartment complex now bae. Why you sounding like you got an attitude for doe?" I ask.

"Well, first you been gone all day. And two, nigga I'm hungry as fuck," she says.

"Chill ma, I got a plate for you that my grams made, when I was at her crib," I said to her.

"Humm, I'm glad she thought bout me, cause I was just bout to say, 'Did you wanna go somewhere and get something to eat?'" she says.

"Well, ain't no need now. I already mashed and I brought this plate for you. So come on bae, so we can go home and you can eat," I say.

"Here I come," she tells me. Then hangs up. I get in the passenger seat, when she comes to get in. "Why you ain't drive bae?" she says.

"I'm chilling a nigga been whipping all day," I say.

"Yea, don't get comfortable in this cuz you definitely got yo own wheels."

"Damn so I can't push yo ride?" I say.

"Nigga a bitch be having moves to makes," she tells me. Changing the CD.

"When you start having moves to make?" I ask her.

"When you got locked up," she says.

"So you being funny right?" I ask her.

"No, I'm just sayin' you was gone and I had to do me."

"What's dat?" I say.

"Now you all up in mines," she says. Turning up the music ...

I just laugh at her. Letting her win.

I put her phone on her lap, pulling mines out my pocket.

"What kind of phone you got?" she ask.

"Dis lil LG 3 joint, Android type shit."

"Yeah dat touch screen game shit. Good so, now you won't be needing mines," she says.

"Yo mom called you I had went over there to see her. And my grams, said why haven't you been to see her in a min?" I say.

"Awww I see grams miss me, I need to go see her too cause it's been a while since I step thru to her crib," she says.

"She said make sure she get her plate back bae. I'll just take it over there tomorrow tho," I say.

"Did you see yo moms and sisters yet?" she ask me.

"Yeah, I'm glad that they was all at my grandma's house too."

"You good bae, you don't need nothin' from the store before we go in?" she asked.

"Yeah pull up to the gas station. I'ma put some gas in here for you and grab something to drink," I say. "You want something bae?" I say getting out the car.

"Just get me some cigarettes, and something to drink," she says to me.

I finish pumping the gas. And see my man Ray pull up and get out his car. "What's up Face, when you get out?" he says.

"Dis morning, what's good wit you doe?" I say.

"Shit man, I got a lil bit of kush I'm fucking wit."

"Oh yeah, dat's what's up," I say.

"We gotta get you in the studio my nigga, I know you got some fire ready," he says.

"You already know I got something in the archives," I tell him.

"Come on bae I'm ready to get home so I can eat," Vic says.

"Aight here I come," I tell her.

"What's up Vicky?" Ray says to her.

"Hey Ray, what's up?" she replied.

"I know you happy your man home."

"And you know dis," she says.

"Aight, bruh," I say embracing him.

"It's on bro," he says.

"What's your number?" I ask him. He tells me the number, then tells me to get at him. "It's a bet bruh," I say, then get in the car and head home wit my lady.

We get home and I grab the drinks and Vicky's plate. As she opens the door. "Here you go bae," I say, handing her the plate. I close and lock the door. She's heating the plate up. "Bae after you eat, we might as well straighten this house out," I say.

"Humm um," she says wit a mouth full of food.

I sit on the couch and start freaking a Mild. "I guess we'll have to bring the TV, in the room out here til we get another one for the living room," I say.

She sit down beside me eating her food, and says, "Bae I told you don't worry bout dat."

"Why shouldn't I?" I say.

"Cause I already got one in lay-a-way for us. I was tryna have it out before you got home," she says.

"How much you need to get it out?" I ask her.

"Another one hundred fifty dollars," she tells me.

"I'll give it to you tomorrow," I say. She finishes her meal. And bout time we're done cleaning and straightening the house it's late out. We just put a movie in and cuddle up.

Before we can get to the middle of the movie, I find myself wit my tongue in the center of my woman's juice box loving the way she taste. After we're done making love, we sleep the rest of the night away.

"Good night," she tells me.

"Good night baby," I say.

CHAPTER 11

I wake up the next morning, get in the shower, brush my teeth, freak one of my Black-n-Milds. Vicky's still asleep looking like she's having a good dream. After getting dress, I light the Black and grab my phone and head to the living room.

I see I have missed calls from, Five, Junie, and A.D. I call them back and tell them I was sleep. But I'm up now and I will see what's up wit 'em when I step out. I log their numbers in my phone. Then I sit back and start to set up my Facebook page. I was hearing about it when I was in the County, and told myself I was gonna make a page when I got out.

I hear Vicky getting up to go to the bathroom. "Morning bae," I say to her.

"Morning boo," she says. Then walks into the bathroom and shuts the door. I'm scrolling thru people's pages seeing who I know. When she walks out and stands in front of me.

"What you doing up so early?" she says.

"Nothing I'm just use to being up early, after being in that damn County," I say.

"I see you couldn't wait to make you a page," she says.

"Chill, why you all on my line?" I ask her. "You got one, right?"

"Umm hmm," she says.

"Okay den so why you sweating me?" I say.

35

"Nigga cause you only on there for them ho's," she says.

"It's too early for dat bae," I say.

"Whatever," she says. And walks away, back to the room.

I sit back put the Mild in the ash tray, and continue to scroll thru my page. I send friend request to a few people and log out.

"Bae?" Vicky yells.

"Huh boo," I say.

"Come here and lay wit me for a lil bit," she says. I walk to the room where she's laying and I lay down next to her. I'm holding her in my arms. And she says, "I missed you holding me like this when you were gone."

I said, "I missed having you next to me like this too."

I doze off wit Vicky til about 11:00 a.m. I wake up, and she's cooking breakfast with the CD player on singing 'Body Party' by Ciera. "I see who's feeling good," I say. "What you making?"

"Just sit down your plate getting made now," she tells me.

I sit, she gives me my plate. "Hum bae, I see you den learned how to cook when I was gone," I say to her.

"Be quiet and eat, you always saying something," she says.

"You know I'm just messing wit you bae, give me a kiss," I say. "Muuahhh!"

We're done eating, I get up to call Strong, to see what's good for da day. And to tell him I'm bout to get in touch wit my mans and see what's up wit dat work for him. "Yo, come scoop me bro," I say.

"Aight where you at?" he says.

"I'm on Hamilton bro call me when you on da street my nigga."

"I'ma be dere in like 20 mins," he says to me and hangs up.

"Face, I'm bout to go get Kimberly, and then I'm going to get some stuff for the house," Vicky says.

"Aight," I say, throwing my clothes on.

"Where you bout to go?" she ask me.

"Strong coming to scoop me," I tell her.

"Well you still gone give me the money for the TV, right?"

"Yeah I got you let me make dis flip today and I got you," I say to her.

"Aight humm," she says giving me a kiss. "I'm out," she says.

"Aye stop and get me a key made too while you're out in traffic," I tell her.

"Okay I will," she says.

"I love you boo."

"Love you too."

Ring, ring, ring ... "Yooo what's up?" I say into the phone.

"Which house is it bro?"

"I'm looking out the window, keep coming down the street bro," I say. "Aight, pull in right here at this white house on yo left. I'm coming out," I said, then hung up.

I'm locking the door to the house walking out to Strong's car. When my phone rings ... "Yo hello?" I said, as I got into Strong's whip.

"Hey boo, I see you home," the person says.

"Who is dis?" I ask. "Nikki! Oh word. How you get my line?" I say to her.

"Why I can't have it nigga?" she says.

"Naw I'm just saying."

"Yea okay, well A.D. just give it to me. I seen him at the store, and asked bout you and he told me you got home yesterday. Then gave me yo number," she says.

"It ain't like you was checking for me when I was in the County. So why you on it now?" I ask.

"Don't play wit me," she says.

"Shidd it's real doe, you said fuck a nigga when I was just sitting it down."

"Well you home now and I wanna make it up to you," she tells me.

"Yeah we'll see I'ma hit you in a min doe," I tell her.

"You betta call me too," she says.

"Yup," I say, and hang up.

"What's good?" Strong says.

"Shit man, I can't call it," I said. "Let me call my mans and see what's up." I dial the number, the phone rings a few times before someone picks up. "Yo 2 cups?"

The person says, "Yo, Bang what's poppin' bruh? Who dis?"

"Face bruh."

"What's poppin' 5, when you touch down?"

"Yesterday bruh, you still in the city doe my nigga?"

"Same spot my nigga swing thru."

"Bet 5."

"Bet," he says. Then we hang up.

"Bro go to Kenwood, so I can see what's up wit dis nigga," I tell Strong.

"Aight bro," he says.

We turn on Bang's street, and it's cars lined up outside his house like it's a block party on the Fourth of July. Strong says, "Man this dude's crib is booming."

"Yeah," I say. "Park right here bro," I tell Strong.

Strong says, "See what you can get for seven hundred fifty dollars," giving me the money.

"Aight I got you," I say to him as I get out da car.

Knock, knock ... "Who dat?" I can hear Bang say.

"Face bruh," I yell.

"You here already?" Bang says to me.

"Shidd, I only live around the corner. I just move over dis way before I got out," I tell him.

As I'm walking thru the kitchen to the living room, I see two young niggas packing up some work. They speak. "What up bruh?"

"What's good?" I say. Then one of 'em gets up and serve the feins that's standing waiting to get their day's fix.

Bang says to me when we get in the living room, "What you get jammed up for nigga?"

"Driving under suspension, and some fucking possession of weed bullshit."

"Oh word!"

"Hell yeah, my nigga, dat shit was crazy," I say.

"We was post to get up that night too," Bang tells me.

"I know man, I was about to turn up at the powerhouse dat night," I say. "Aye doe bruh, what dem gezzys of da food going for?" I say to him.

He tells me, "Bruh I would usually let 'em go for one hundred fifty dollars a gee, but you can give me a hunnid."

"Aight, what it's looking like?" I say to him.

He grabs a plate from under the couch. He says, "This that fire too my nigga. Yo phone ain't gone stop ringing I'm telling you."

"Shidd, umm let me get five grizzys my nigga," I say to Bang. Giving him five hundred dollars.

I think to myself, 'Like damn,' wondering how much do Strong be getting from his people for the whole seven hundred fifty dollars?

"Here you go bro," Bang says giving me the work.

"Aight bet my nigga. I'ma get wit you ASAP, when I need some more bruh," I say.

"Aight," he says to me as we embrace.

I say, "It's on y'all" to the young boys Bang has packing up the dope.

"Stay safe out dere bro," they tell me. And I walk out the door.

"Humm bruh," I say to Strong as I get into the car.

He said, "Yo what's this Face?"

"Five grams, oh yeah here go a C-note back too bro," I say.

"Good looking bruh, shit if it's that fire I'ma be fucking wit you."

I said, "He says it's official. So let me know."

"Aye bro, take me to holla at my pops. I gotta check on my car bro."

Strong says, "Where he stay off Parkman St. still?"

"Yup." As we're riding to my pop's spot I log into my Facebook page. It's friend request from damn near everybody in my city. I accept everyone I fuck wit. Then I post a status and look thru my news feeds, and I see this picture of Vicky and I kissing. It's a pic we took before I violated probation. "Look at this muthafucka already bro," I say to Strong.

He sees the pic and said, "You already know how Vic is. You out know too so she definitely about to act a fool."

I peep the caption she wrote: 'Yeah my nigga out, so y'all ho's betta know ya place.' I put a like on the pic and comment.

Then I check my inbox, I notice I got a message. It's from Nikki. It says, 'You betta call me later too ugly.' I message her back: 'LOL. I see you on a nigga doe, SMH I'ma hit you up doe.' I send the message then I take a selfie, post it then log out.

I call Victoria's phone, as we're pulling into my pop's driveway. "Hold up right quick bruh," I say to Strong as I hop out his car.

"Hello," Vicky says.

"Yo bae you real funny," I say. "I seen yo pic you posted of us already starting shit."

She said, "What nigga I ain't allowed?"

"I'm not saying dat boo, but dang ma let a nigga breathe a lil. Nah I'm just messing wit you baby," I say.

"Yeah cause, I was bout to say you got me fucked up nigga. You mines I don't give a fuck."

"You funny bae. But anyways, what you doing?" I ask as I knock on my pop's door.

"Nothin' just finish shoppin' bout to drop this stuff off then head back to Kim's."

"Bro you got some more smoke?" I can hear Kim saying in the background.

"Tell her I'ma come thru in a min." My pops open the door I walk in. "Baby I'm bout to get off here tho, I was just checking on you," I tell her.

"Where you at?" she ask.

"My dad's crib."

"When you coming over Kim's?"

"After I stop and see Rayn."

"Aight boo, talk to you in a min."

"Aight love you."

"Love you more," she says, and we hang up.

"Boy what's up you aight?" my pops says.

"I'm good, just tryna shake back," I tell him.

"I heard you got out yesterday. Why you just now stopping by here?" he says.

"I had to make moves pops you already know how it is."

"Yeah making moves got you locked up too."

I said, "Pops chill man we den had this talk a million times when I was just sitting it down."

"Aight son I'm just telling you," he says.

"Hi Face," his girlfriend walks in and says to me.

"How you doing?" I said to her, giving her a hug.

"I'm okay," she says. "How about you?"

"Just tryna make it," I say to her.

"Well, you looking good baby stay out of trouble. You hear me?"

"I will," I say, as she's walking out of the kitchen.

"Aight we gone see. And don't be acting like no stranger either," she yells back to me.

"Yo pops, where the car keys to my truck?"

"Let me grab 'em real quick," he says.

"Aight I'm bout to run out here and tell my ride he can leave."

"Aye Strong, I'm about to get in the truck bro."

"Aight bro, hit me up later I got some plays to make. My phone jumping," he says.

"It's a bet bruh. Oh let me know what dat shit like too bro," I say.

"Aight bet," he says and pulls out the driveway.

CHAPTER 12

"Here goes the keys son," Pops says, "It's in the back behind the garage. I'm move my car so you can get out the driveway."

I say, "Aight good looking for holding it down for me too pops."

I walked around to the back yard, behind the garage and see my black and gold Eddie B. Edition Expedition. 'Damn my ride needs a wash,' I think to myself. I hop in and start her up. She starts right up, I hit gas a couple times. Then I shift the gears into drive, and come around the garage onto the driveway pavement.

I roll the window down and tell my dad I'ma give him a call later, and that I'm bout to head to the car wash.

He says, "Okay son be careful." And be sure to go reinstate my license.

I beep the horn and pull out, thinking like, 'Yeah I do gotta call down to the license bureau. And check on how much I'ma have to pay to get my L's back.'

I'm cleaning out the inside of my car before, I go thru the automatic wash. I see I still got my tire shine, interior spray, and some towels to dry with. I get to the back driver side passenger door, and I see the scratches Vicky ass put there before I got violated and locked up.

'It isn't that bad,' I think to myself, but the shit pisses me off knowing it's there. I finish vacuuming the back seat and floor. And get inside and go thru the car wash. I'm looking thru the middle console and glove compartment, looking for my CD's.

I come across some old receipts and pictures. I stop when I come across a picture of me and my homies in this bar we use to chill at called 'The Cliffs.' I put the pic back, and grab my CD case I was searching for.

I'm flipping thru the CD's, I see my Trill Fam CD 'All or Nothing,' and put the disc in the deck. My phone rings ... Ring, ring, ring ... "Yo who dis?"

Five said, "Yo 5 it's me nigga. Where you at?"

I say, "Oh what's good? I'm at the car wash. I just got the truck from pop's crib."

Five says, "Oh aight bruh dis nigga Junie said do yo got some more of dat loud?"

"I'ma hit y'all in a min bruh," I said.

"Aight whore," Five says.

"Mighty," I say.

"Mighty," he said. And we hang up.

I finish drying the truck off, wiping down the dashboard, and interior. I'm finishing wit the tire shine when I peep I need some air in my tires. 'Damn I gotta stop at Rayn's and the gas station,' I think to myself.

I'm calling Rayn's phone on my way to get the air in my tires ...

"Hello," Rayn says.

"Yeah what up bro," I say.

Rayn says, "What's up bro?"

I say, "Shit me I'm tryna get the same thing as yesterday."

He said, "You know I'm bout to head to work. Where you at?"

I said, "I'm bout to pull into the gas station across from Sav A Lot. I gotta get some air in my tires."

He says, "Aight bro I'm bout to pull up in five mins."

"Bet," I said.

"Aight," he says.

I'm done putting air in the tires. And I walk into the store and grab some Milds and a deuce-deuce of Colt 45. I walk out the store and I see Rayn pulling up to a pump.

I hop in the car with him. I said, "What's up bro?"

He said, "Shit bro bout to hit the work site. Here bro, dis just a lil zip."

I say, "What's the ticket?"

"Just give me two hundred twenty-five dollars," he tells me.

I grab the two hundred twenty-five dollars out my pocket count it out and give it to 'em. I said, "Good looking bruh."

He says, "I thought you were coming up to try and see what's up wit you getting a job?"

"I'ma try and get to it sometime this week," I say.

He says, "Don't be bullshitting Face I'm telling you I can probably get you in."

I say, "Aight bro I'ma shoot thru."

"Aight," he said. Then we dap one another up and I hop out to get into my truck.

I'm sitting in the truck talking to Vicky on the phone. I said, "Bae do Kim still want dat?"

Vicky says, "Yeah where you at?"

"I'm on da North," I tell her.

She says, "Well come to McDonald's right quick cause I'm on my way to the East Side."

I said, "I'm bout to be there in a few mins," and we end the call.

I'm pulling in McDonald's calling Five back from earlier. Ring, ring ...

He answers, "Yo."

"Five what's good?" I say, "Where you at?"

He says, "I'm at my sister's in the T-homes."

I tell him, "Aight I'm bout to swing thru," and to tell Junie I got dat smoke too,

"It's on 5," he says.

"Yup," I tell him and hang up.

I park next to Vicky, and hop in her car in the back seat. I say, "What's up?" to Kim and Vicky.

They both speak, and hand me a fifty. I put her a nice ti ti together and give her ten dollars back. Kim says, "Thanks bro."

"You welcome ugly," I say to her.

Vicky says, "Bae what you bout to do?"

I said, "Nothin' bout to go see who can fix that dumb ass scratch you put on my door."

She has a perplexed look on her face. Then says, "Bae that's so old. Why you even bring that up?"

I tell her, "I'm just messing wit you boo. But I ain't bout to do nothing doe, just see what's good wit my lil niggas for a min. Where y'all about to go on the East?"

She says, "Meet Wiggy at yo gram's crib."

"I'ma see you in a min then bae," I say.

"Love you," she says.

I tell her, I love her too. We exchange kisses, and I hop out. "Call me when you leave from my grandma's," I tell her. And close the door.

I turn up the volume on my system. And Trill Fam's 'Ducked Off' comes thru the speakers. I turn in the T's to see Five and Junie in front of his sister's apartment.

I pull up they hop in, and we sliding thru the T's "It's dead as fuck out here."

Five says, "Hell yeah bro it use to be jumping out here back in the day before I went and did the two years in juvi."

I said, "Hell yeah bruh. But da Hamps use to really be popping, dat's where dem ho's was at."

Junie said, "Man it's cold as fuck out here y'all really think somebody bout to be outside? Fuck no," he says. We all laugh at his comment. Somehow I managed to find myself on Brier St., parked in front of A.D.'s mom's crib.

Junie says, "Yo Face let me see what dat fire looking like."

I say, "Dis dat medical shit bruh same as the other shit I gave you."

He sees it and says, "Hell yeah bro let me get a quarter for da hunnid my nigga."

I said, "I really need a buck twenty but you good doe."

I put the quarter together for him and gives it to him, and he gives me the big face hunnid. Junie starts rolling up ASAP.

Five says, "Bro let's slide to the store I need a Mild."

I say, "I got some," and hands the pack.

He's freaking the Black, Junie's rolling up, and I drinking my Colt 45. When I see lil cuz Dre and my lil nigga Champ, coming out da house.

"Who dat?" Dre says.

I rolled down the window, and said, "Face, lil bruh what's up?"

"Oh shit Face what's up cuz?"

"Shit bruh."

Champ says, "What's good bro?"

"Same shit y'all already know," I say.

Dre says, "A.D. told me he seen you yesterday."

I said, "Word cuz?"

He says, "Hell yeah."

So now it's me, Dre, Champ, Five, and Junie all sitting in the truck. They're all smoking on da loud, I'm just chilling hitting the Black. Strong calls, ask me did I ever get some more smoke. I said, "Yeah bruh what's up?"

He gives me this number and tell me to call it they tryna spend.

I say, "Who am I asking for?"

He tells me, "Just call 'em I'm good."

"Aight bro good looking," I say.

He says, "Yup," then hangs up.

I dial the number he gives me. It rings a few times no one answer. I end the call and my line ring right away. I can see it's the number I just called so I answer. "Hello ...," I say.

"Umm hello, you just call my phone?" the female says.

I said, "Yeah dis Face you ..."

"Oh fa real, why you just now calling me?" the girl says.

I said, "Who dis yo?"

She says, "Terria nigga you don't know my voice yet?"

I tell her, "I just met you yesterday ma. What's up doe?"

She says, "You got some smoke?"

"Yup," I say to her.

"Where you at?" she says.

"I'm East bound," I tell her.

She says, "Me too, meet me on Columbia St. in da circle."

"Aight I'ma be dere in a lil second," I say to her.

She says, "Okay," and we hang up.

"Aye what's up, what y'all bout to do?" I ask everybody.

"I'm wit you bro," Five says.

"I'm staying at the crib cuz," Dre says. Champ stays with Dre. And Junie wants to get drop off at some chick's crib a couple streets over.

I drop Junie off. He says he'll hit me up in a lil while. I tell him, "It's a bet," then me and Five slide out.

CHAPTER 13

"What's up shawty?" I said to Terria as she opens the door and gets in the back.

She said, "Nigga what I tell you about that shawty shit?"

"Dat's just how a nigga talk baby girl, my bad ma," I say.

She said, "Yeah okay you already know I don't like dat doe why you talking bout yo bad?"

I said, "Whatever ma. But what's up doe? Oh yeah dis my mans Five, Five dis Terria."

They both acknowledge one another, then Terria says, "My cusin over here and wanna know what's up on an eighth?"

I say, "Tell 'em it's going for sixty dollars."

She said, "Aight let me see it right quick." As I'm putting it together, she says, "Whose car is this you driving? It's nice."

I said, "Who's driving?" and I pass her the smoke.

She says, "Umm I guess you in traffic nigga. Hold up I'll be right back."

"Aight," I say.

"Yo Five, what you think about dat book?"

He looks out the window at her, and says, "Nigga you ain't read dat yet?"

I said, "Naw I just met her yesterday at my homie's crib."

48

He says, "She right bro let me know when you get a couple of chapters into dat."

"If the first few pages ain't no good you already know how I do bro," I say.

We're laughing, when she opens the door. She hands me the money and says, "That better be some fire too don't be having me call you for no bullshit."

I say, "It's the same from yesterday."

She said, "Yeah right. Well hit me up 'when you get right' like you said the other day." She's quoting what I told her yesterday.

I said, "Yeah I got you shawty."

She and Five, tells each other bye. Then she hops out the truck making the 'call me' sign with her hand.

"Yeah Face, you gotta dig in that bruh," Five tells me.

"You ain't lying my nigga," I tell him. "And she's on my line too. But I gotta get to this money right now doe," I say, then turn up the music.

We're in traffic, going down Laird Ave., when a notification from my Facebook comes thru on my phone. I see it's a post on my wall from my older cusin Tony. He's saying, "What's up lil bruh, I'm glad to know you're home. Jail ain't no place for a real nigga bro get back at me. '74 til the world blow cuz.'" He's a Gangster Disciple better known as G.D..

I hit him back and said, "Man you know it's '22-12 all is well cuz.' Almighty don't like nobody. What's up doe fam?" So we're messaging back and forth for a min, and end up telling each other we're gonna link up soon. I send my condolences to him and the fam. And tell him to tell Aunt Crystol, I'ma be calling her later today when I get to the house.

Then I log out and put the phone down. Five says, "Yo lord, pull into BP right fast."

I said, "We need some gas too I don't know why I ain't get none earlier."

We enter the store and I see, Mica working the register. That's my partner 'C-No's' sister. (RIP my nigga!) "Hey bro what's up?" she says.

"Shit sis what's good?" I say.

She said, "Shit man just tryna keep my spirits up. You know ever since dat happen wit bro."

I said, "I already know sis you just gotta stay strong and be the best you can be for yo kids and the fam. Feel me?"

"Yeah man, I'm trying dis shit hurt doe," she says.

"I feel it trust me, dat was my dog," I tell her. "How Shanna and Ma Dukes holding up?"

She said, "They cool, but you know mom fucked up tho that was her baby."

I say, "More less sis. What's up wit pops?"

She tells me, "He's out the way at their people's house. He's good tho."

I say, "Dat's what's up hit me up sometime." I give her my number, and tell her to tell Shanna to get at me.

I pay for my gas, and Five's ordering his stuff as I go outside to pump the gas. Five's come out the store opens the car door, and says, "Bruh yo phone's ringing."

I said, "Answer it bruh." Ring, ring, ring ... I hear the phone.

"Yooo," Five saying as, he picks up the call. "Yeah who dis?" he says. "Oh alright, hold up right quick." Five said, "Here bro it's Shawn."

I said, "Good looking," as I grab the phone. "Hello what's up nigga?" I say.

Shawn said, "What's up cuz?"

"Nothing man at the gas station filling up the truck."

He says, "Oh word you went and got yo 1's back bruh,"

I say, "Hell naw man I need to doe. A.D. gave you my number cuz?"

Shawn says, "Yup I just talk to him before I called you, he said he about to put some bread on my books."

"Yeah he got it shidd dat nigga shot me two hundred fifty dollars yesterday. I told him to tell you I got you when I get right. You feel me?"

He says, "You good bro I know you got me. I'm cool right now neways you just got out."

"What's good wit dat nigga Oz?"

Shawn tells me, "Man Oz done flip'ed out last night and went to the hole."

"How da hell dat pop off cuz?" I say.

Shawn tell me, "You know dat ho ass C.O. Walkins, whatever the fuck his name is?"

"Yeah I know who you talking bout cuz," I say.

He said, "Well they come in and did a shakedown. Walkins ho ass goes in Oz's cell and starts tearing all he pics off the walls and stepping on all his cards his girl be sending him. You know he be having them joints designed around his floor and shit. Then flushes this nigga's food that he was making down the toilet."

I say, "Damn, so what bro do?"

He tells me, "That nigga flip'ed start calling 'em bitches and just wilding bruh."

I said, "Shidd I would of too bruh dat ho ass bitch Walkins just be fucking wit muthafuckas."

Shawn says, "Cuz who was dat that picked up yo phone?"

I tell him, "That was Five."

"Oh word cuz put him on the phone," he says.

"Five dis nigga Shawn want you," I say, giving him the phone. I hang the pump back up and close the gas cap on my gas tank, then hop in the car. They're choppin' it up on the phone, while I freak a Mild before I pull out.

I hear Five saying, "Hit us back later."

I can tell the call is bout to end so I yell into the phone, "And tell Shawn to keep his head up."

I'm bout to pull out the store parking lot when I see, Vicky's car pulling in. She pulls up besides me and gets out and comes around to my side of the car. I roll down the window. I said, "Don't be blowing down on me like dat yo."

Vicky says, "I wish you would of had somebody in here so I could act the fuck up. Naw but, what's up you got dat bread bae, so I can go up here and drop dat on the TV?"

I said, "Yeah," counting out one hundred fifty dollars for her. "Bae did you go get the key made yet?"

She said, "No but I'm going to after I leave from here. Then I'm gonna go put this down on the TV."

I said, "How you gonna get the TV to the crib?"

She says, "They gone deliver it to the house for us. What you bout to do?" she ask me.

I said, "Shit fa real bout to shoot up here to Midas, and get an oil change. Then I'm dropping bruh off and meeting you at the crib bae."

"Okay love you," she says.

"Yup love you too," I said. "Muahhh," we kiss and I pull out heading to Midas.

Five says, "Face bruh you tryna step out tonight?"

I said, "Fa real bruh we can depending on what wifey wanna do. You know a nigga just got out so you know she gone be all on a nigga's back. You feel me?"

He said, "You already know Vic ain't having dat shit unless she coming wit you."

"Nigga please I run dat shit bro don't get it twisted," I say.

Five said, "Bro quit fronting my nigga. Only time she ain't got you on lock is when you upset with her." I was about to say something, until we were interrupted by the service guy who working on the truck.

The service guy says, "You're all done here sir?"

I said, "How much would that be again?"

He says, "Umm it'll be thirty-nine dollars and seventy-nine cents. Is there anything else I can help you wit sir?"

I said, "Yeah man let me get two of them car fresheners, the green everfresh joints."

He says, "That'll be forty-three dollars and twenty-nine cents." I give him a fifty, he rings me up gives me my change. And says, "Thanks for coming to Midas."

I said, "Aight." He opens the garage door and I pull out.

"Aye bro, where you tryna go to?" I say to Five.

He said, "Shidd man take me to my brother's crib in the Hamps."

"Aight," I say, and turn the music up as I pull out in traffic.

"Five's phone rings, and I turn down the music a lil. "What's up Fats?" he says, into the phone. I can't hear what Fats is saying but, from what Five says I can tell they're talking about meeting up at the club tonight. He's talking for a few more mins then hangs up, and says, "Shidd bro you gotta come out tonight my nigga it's jumping off tonight at the Cliff's."

I turn into the Hamps and, tell him I'ma call 'em and let him know what's up.

He says, "Dat's what's up Five." Then tells me to make a left in the first parking lot to my left. I pull in and we peace each other up and, he proceeds to get out.

I said, "Almighty bruh."

"All is well lord, hit me up if you coming out," he says. Then shuts the door.

I egress, out the parking lot and head home to my crib.

CHAPTER 14

I pull into my driveway and park my truck next to Vicky's car. I knock on the door to our house, and think like, 'Damn I hope she got my key made and didn't forget bout it."

Vicky opens the door, "Hey bae," she says.

I said, "What's up boo did you get the house key made for me?"

She says, "Yes bae it's on the end table in the living room." I shut the door behind me, and she walks into the living room.

When I step into the living room she says, "Do you like the TV?"

"Yeah ma, it's straight. It looks good to me." I grab my key off of the table and attach it to my key ring with my other keys.

I sit down next to Vicky and ask her how her day's been.

She said, "It's been aight I just did a lil shopping for the house, chilled wit Kim and yo Aunt Wiggy, seen yo grandma, paid for the new TV, and got ya key made. What bout you?" she says.

"Nothing really just been in traffic tryna boom a lil. Dis shit slow as fuck fa real fucking wit dis green."

She said, "Well don't go doing nothing stupid cause you just got out. Ain't no need to be in a rush for dat shit."

I said, "Man you sound silly as fuck bae I gotta get it. I'm tryna stun for the summer. Plus Christmas is coming up. I know yo spoiled butt wants something nice."

She said, "Yeah but I want you out here wit me. I don't need you locked up no more I missed you long enough."

I want to tell her bout my plans for the night but, I keep 'em to myself.

She asks me if I am hungry.

I said, "Yeah bae."

She said. "What do you want me to make our favorite?"

I say, "What taco salad," knowing that's what she's talking about.

"Umm hmm," she says.

I said, "Yeah it's cool it's something you can whip up. Plus a nigga ain't had that in a lil min."

When she gets up, I ask, "What's this you're watching boo?"

She said, "Oh it's nothing fa real bae you can turn it."

Well, I'm flicking thru the channels I think about my strap. Man where the hell are my guns, her ass ain't said nothing about my shit since I been out. I yell to Vicky, "Yo bae, where the hell is my Tech Lugar and Calico .45 at?"

She says, "Huh?"

I put down the remote and walk into the kitchen. "I said, where is my guns at bae?"

She says, "Now bae you already know Rayshawn," that's her other brother, "came and got the Tech Lugar."

I said, "Yeah aight, but where is the four-five doe?"

She said, "Face, don't be mad but somebody stole it."

I said, "How da fuck did someone steal my shit Victoria?"

"When I was moving, well packing up at the old house the day before I moved here. A few people were over and it came up missing."

"Vicky, man I swear you're forever messing up or fucking wit some shit that belong to me," I said, "So why ain't you tell me this when I was in the County?"

She says, "Cause I ain't want you to be mad. Look at you, you tripping now."

I said, "You would be salty too about yo shit."

"I'm sorry boo just calm down doe please."

"Man I'm cool yo, but look doe call 'Cleave,'" that's her brother's nickname, "and tell him I need da Tech."

I go back into the living room take my weed out of my pocket and my bread, and put it on the living room table. I go into the room and grab a Mild out of the pack I had at the house from yesterday.

When I get back in the living room. Vic yells, and tells me her brother's in Cleveland but he got me when he gets back.

I said, "Aight," and freak my Mild, thinking like, 'Damn I hate stepping out without my heat on me.'

I'm smoking my Mild, watching 'Gangland on the Vicelords.' They're talking bout Willie Lloyd, and how the A.V.L.N., began in 1958. When Vicky walks in with my plate.

She says, "Bae, here is your plate I'm bout to grab you a pop out of the refrigerator. Or do you want a beer?"

"A soda will be cool," I tell her.

She comes wit the drinks and, her plate. Sits down next to me and, asks me, am I mad bout my pistol.

I said, "Yeah you know I'm salty bout my shit but it's cool tho bae. Just answer me this question. Who helped you move, well pack our shit?"

She names a few people, then says that she doesn't really think that it came up missing then tho.

"So when do you believe it went missing Vicky?" I ask.

She says, she thinks Troub got it, or one of his friends. Because they were over at the old house before we moved and saw it.

Vicky says, that they were beefing wit some young five-star niggas, and were talking bout they needed some straps. And then when she was moving, the pistol was missing.

I say, "So why didn't you say this in the beginning bae?"

"Because you know how you are, you always blow things outta proportion when we talk about stuff."

"Well it's just how you communicate that has me like that. But don't worry bout it just tell Troub, I need to holla at him."

She gives me a kiss, and we finish eating. I guess she's glad I'm not tripping.

The 'Gangland' episode goes off I finish eating, and take my dishes to the kitchen sink. I'm walking back thru the living room when Vicky's phone rings, she presses the 'end' button sending the caller to voicemail.

"Why don't you answer yo phone?" I ask.

"Cause I'm not done eating," she tells me, "and it probably wasn't shit anyways."

I say, "You better keep dem niggas in check. Don't let me find out no bullshit."

"Boy bye! Ain't no niggas calling me, dey already know what's up."

"Come on, Vicky who do you think you're talking to?" I say, going into the room.

"Whatever," she says.

'Oh shit let me go get my phone, before she is all in my shit,' I think to myself knowing her ass. Like I thought, I walk in and she's got my phone in her hand tryna get on my Facebook page.

I take my phone from her. "Damn let me guess. I can't put my phone down and leave it around you without you all up in my shit?"

She says, "You already know how I am. But you must have something to hide or you wouldn't be worried."

"What the hell I got to hide and I just got out?"

She says, "I ain't tryna hear it whatever. Let me get some of that weed doe."

I said, "Don't take all of my shit," and went back to the back to lay back. Being out all day running around got me tired. But I think that taco salad is what did it for real.

So as I'm lying down, I zoned out for a little bit for about an hour and a half. When I get up it's 9:00 at night, I get out of bed, and go to the bathroom.

I turn on the shower, and adjust the water how I like it. I step into the water, and I'm washing up thinking about my gear and what I'm bout to wear tonight.

I hop out of the shower, and dry off.

I walk out of the bathroom and I see Vicky asleep on the couch. I'm like, 'Hell yeah let me hurry up and slide. So I don't gotta hear her mouth.'

In the room, I'm looking thru my clothes tryna figure out what I'ma wear. I settle for a white Polo collar shirt, my brand new black Tru Religion jeans, that I bought before I got locked up. And some white, black, and red Polo boots that I only wore once.

I spray some Axe body spray on, put on my clothes, and look in the mirror like, 'Damn dat boy fresh.' Then I take a dab of my Ed Hardy cologne and rub it on my neck and wrist. I get my phone off of the charger, and see that I have three missed calls and a notification update.

"Where you going Face?" I hear Vicky say from behind.

I turn around and see her wit her hand on her hip. I say, that I'm bout to step out.

She says, "So you were just going to leave without telling me?"

"I was going to tell you before I left bae."

"How long are you going to be gone boo?" she says.

"Not long I'm only stepping out wit the team then coming back home," I tell her.

"Face fa real don't be out all night, and you better come home too," she tells me.

"Bae chill you know I'm coming back to the crib."

"Well I'm probably bout to go chill wit Kimberly for a lil til you come in. Cause I hate being here by myself."

I tell her, "Okay," and kiss her on the forehead then the lips.

I grab my leather Steelers jacket and my Steelers hat, go into the living room. I grab my money off of the table, and my weed. Then think like, 'Damn I hate going out without my gun on me. I hope these niggas got the cannon wit 'em in case something pop off.'

I pick up my keys, and my Mild out of the ash tray. Yell to Vicky, to let her know that I'm bout to leave.

She's in the shower. She tells me to lock the door, and that she loves me.

I say, okay and that I love her too, then head out of the door to my truck.

I'm in the truck, calling back my missed calls. One of 'em is from Bang calling tryna get up wit me, I tell him to meet me at the Cliffs.

He says, he'll be there he's bout to make a stop to get some loud first tho.

I let him know I got some.

Bang says, "It's a bet," and he'll be at the bar in bout an hour.

I say, "Bet." And we end the call.

I'm backing out of the driveway, calling the last person back from my missed calls. The phone's ringing ...

"Hello bro what's up?" It's my sister Niecy.

I say, "Yo what's up sis?"

"Man bruh why weren't you answering, dis ho ass nigga was just out here hollering?" she says.

"Who are you talking about?" I said.

She tells me it's this dude that goes by the name, 'Chino.'

It doesn't register at the moment. Then it hits me that's one of these lames, I got into it wit bout three and a half years ago. I say, "Yo where the hell are you at sis?"

She said, she in the Hamps but Chino already left. And that he was hollering bout it's my nigga's fault that his brother passed, and that I'ma ho.

I only beat him up that night we fought cause he was drunk. I say, "Yo I'ma bout to pull up, in two point two!" I tell 'em and, hang up.

CHAPTER 15

I'm riding down Tod Ave. thinking this nigga Chino gone make me burn his dumb ass. First we get into it bout who knows what, matter of fact at a party in my nigga's basement over a fuckin' cigarette. Now this shit, but I really don't think it was over that cig, I always thought that was bout the situation, wit a few niggas I know and his brother.

Truthfully, I believe the police let my nigga die that night. Cause ain't no way they could sit in front of the house all night and not see my homie.

Then in the morning his people find him at the same house the police was at the whole night.

"Shit crazy man, RIP Kamal! 'Y.T. for Life' bruh!"

I'm pulling into the Hamps, it's about 10:45. I see my sisters coming out of this building, that my godbrother stays in. I pull up on 'em and roll the window down.

"Get in," I tell 'em.

"What's up bro?" they both say to me as they climb in.

"Nothin' man bout to go to the Cliffs for a min. What the fuck ol' boy was just trippin' on doe?" I say.

Cherelle says, "I don't know bro, dat nigga was just mugging. So I asked him what he was looking at and he started talking that bullshit."

I say, "Oh word, shit I'ma pull up on dat nigga don't even trip."

"Shidd doe nigga I see you're fresh," Seaniece says.

I respond, "Yeah you know I'm back."

"Boy go on wit your ugly ass hell," she says. They start laughing.

"Yeah that ain't what y'all homegirls be saying," I said.

"Who Sha'Quia?" Relle says and they bust out laughing even more.

"Man where the heck y'all going?" I say, getting irritated wit their bullshit.

They say, "Take us to mommy's bro."

"Aight bet," I say, then head to my mom's crib.

I pull up at my mom's house. It was only around the corner.

"Aight bro, you got some loud?" Relle says.

"Yeah what's good?" I say.

"Shit bro let us get some we ain't bout to keep buying that shit from you nigga. What the fuck, you feel me Niece?" Relle says.

"Umm hmm shidd," Niecy says.

"Y'all got it but don't think this shit sweet doe," I tell 'em. I give em the smoke and tell 'em to tell mommy I love her.

They egress, but on the way out they tell me to be safe. And that they love me.

I say, "You already know," and, that I love them too.

I hit my horn, and pull out of my mother's driveway.

My phone rings ... Ring ... Ring ... I got my favorite Trill Fam song saved as my ringer 'Soft to Hard.' So that's what's playing before I pick up.

"Yooo what's up bruh?" I see that it's Five on the caller ID.

He says, "Nothing man where you at bro?"

"I'm bout to shoot to the Cliffs now, where you at nigga?" I said.

"I'm outside in the parking lot just pulled up wit Bravo," he tells me. Bravo's his brother a cool nigga fa real.

"Aight, I'm bout to be dere bruh. Aye doe nigga you got the cannon on you?" I ask 'em.

Five said, "Man bruh you know I keep nick wit me."

I say, "It's a bet," and hang up. 'I hate not having my pistol on me when I go out,' I think as I bend a few corners on my way to the club.

I'm in the Cliffs' parking lot locking my doors, when I see this nigga Bang pull up in dat royal blue 760 BMW. Wit the 24 inch dubs floating and the blue dust plates in the back.

"Damn dat bitch hard," I say to myself putting my fist over my mouth. I step out of the truck and hit the alarm.

Bang and I embrace one another, then he says, "I see you got the Expedition back on the road."

I say, "Yeah my shit straight but I'm tryna get in one of dem joints bruh."

He looks back at his whip and says, "Yeah dat bitch mean doe. I just got her from a dude in North Carolina that played for the Panthers about two months ago."

I said, "That muthafucka's nice bruh. Let's step in here doe."

Bang hit the alarm on his whip, then we enter into the club. The security pats us down and we proceed to the bar. Five, walks over to us to get to the bar. "Yo Bang dis Five, Five dis Bang," I introduce the two and we order our drinks.

Bang says, "What y'all drinking? First round's on me."

We tell 'em, "It don't matter whatever you're drinking as long as it's white."

"Aight," he says, and gets the waitress' attention.

"Yo Bang we gone be over dere at that table," I tell him. And point in the direction I'm referring to.

Five says, "I didn't think you were coming out bro."

"I don't know why not nigga I wear da pants in my relationship wit my girl," I tell him.

"What's up doe bruh, you bring some smoke wit you?"

"Yeah my nigga," I said.

"Shit roll something up den you still ain't smoking?" he asks me.

"Bro you know I ain't booffing bruh."

"Here man give me something for dis," he says. He hands me thirty dollars, I tighten him up, as Bang sits down beside us.

He bought us a bottle of Grey Goose, and himself a bottle of Pink Moscato. He says, "Dat's all my nigga I'ma fuck wit dis Pink Moscato."

I say, "Bet whore good looking."

Five's already busting down his Swisher, when Bang says, "Face let me see dat smoke you got bruh."

I hand him the bag. He looks at it and says, "Dis dat official, huh bruh?"

I tell him, "Yeah that's that loud pack bruh."

He said, "I can smell it man let me get a quarter outta dat."

"Aight," I tell him. He gives me the fire back and, I eyeball a quake outta what's left of the smoke. I give it to him he hands me one hundred fifty dollars.

"Shidd, bruh I got change dat shit only goes for a buck twenty my nigga," I tell him.

He says, "Man keep dat shit just know where we're at if I need some smoke."

So we're chilling getting our drink on, they're matching one another on the bud. I'm smoking a Mild, when I see Nikki walking in my direction wit one of her cusins wit her.

She steps up to me, and says, "Nigga you ain't shit why ain't you call me?"

I tell her, "I've been busy tryna see dis bread."

"So why are you in here then?"

"Da homies wanted to step out, you feel me?" I said.

She said, "Nah I don't feel you." We look over and see Bang and her people chopping it up. Nikki says, "Damn girl let dat nigga breathe."

I tell her to chill, let my mans work.

"Anyways, what are you getting into after this?"

"I can't call it I'ma definitely hit you up doe," I say to her.

She says, "Well buy a bitch a drink, so I can get out of yo face."

"Dat's all you wanted, I already knew what you were on," I say as I give her a twenty dollar bill.

She says, "No it wasn't I'm tryna be wit you tonight dat's what I'm on."

"We gon see what's up," I say to her.

Nikki says, "Come on girl," to her cusin, "that nigga ain't going nowhere," speaking of Bang.

Bang says, "Aye bruh her people's right. Damn I ain't even get her name. I'ma save her in this muthafucka as 'Foxy.' You know who she is bruh?" Bang asks me.

"I forget her name dat bitch from Cali doe fool," I tell him.

Five passes Bang the blunt and says, "Yeah that's a nice book."

Bang says, "Yeah I'm tryna write that muthafucka."

I think to myself, 'These niggas high as hell.'

I'm looking at the entrance to the club, when I peep Bang's lil niggas that were packing up the work when I was in his trap earlier. "Yo bruh, it looks like the bouncer's giving ya homies a hard time over dere," I tell him.

Bang looks and then was on his way to his feet. But I tell him to chill I got it.

"Aye big dawg," I say to the huge bouncer. "What's the problem these my young homies? They're wit me."

"Oh they here wit you Face?" the security guard says.

"Yeah bro."

"They ain't showed me any ID though man, and the owner's in tonight."

"Look bruh they're good there's not gone be any problems outta my homies. What's the ticket bruh, let my young hittas have fun wit the fellas," I said, handing him a fifty.

He looks and grabs the money and tucks it. Then says, "Aight man, but let me pat y'all down." He searches 'em but doesn't feel the baby 380 caliber hidden in the last one's Timberland boot.

We walk away back to the table, where Bang and Five are chilling still smoking. They say, "Good looking on dat Face."

"I thought I was gone have to bang the nigga out," the one in black says.

"Don't worry about it, I know damn near everybody in here. The owner fucks wit me the long way," I say to 'em. It registers that I don't know their names, but they know mine.

"Yo man what's y'all lil niggas' names, I don't think I got 'em when we met the first time?"

"They call me 'Young,'" the one in the colorful ass Coogi jacket said. He has on some raw Coogi shoes to match his coat.

"And I'm 'Black,' the other one says, wit his black Nascar jacket on wit a black hoodie underneath it that zips all the way up into a full mask.

We got to the table, and Bang says, "Man what y'all doing up here y'all supposed to have the trap jumping?"

Young says, "Big homie we sold all the work so we said fuck it we bout to slide up here and make sure you straight."

"So y'all pushed everything?" Bang asked 'em.

Black says, "Dollar for dollar bruh. It's some major bread out dis way."

"Huh bruh," says Young.

"Dis Face's lil brother Five, Five this is the goons Young and Black," Bang says. They greet each other, and we continue to chop it up for a min. Til the song 'I Love This Shit' remix comes on by August Alsina ft. Trey Songs and Chris Brown.

Five, Young, and Black slide out to the dance floor to get up on some honeys.

"Yo Bang, what are you letting the onions of the food go for?"

"Shidd Face, right now it's sweet I'm letting them go for eighteen hundred dollars a zip. But in the drought, prices can be as high as twenty-three to twenty-five hundred dollars."

"Word bruh! I think I'ma tryna make a move wit you, cause the loud shit is too slow fa real."

Bang says, "Just let me know you know I got you my nigga. But right now I'm bout to get up wit dese hos in here doe, nigga I know you tryna bag something you just got out too."

"I'm cool fa real bruh, I need to get this money," I said.

"We gone most definitely get to dat Face but, enjoy yourself tonight tho," Bang tells me. As he gets up and goes to the dance floor to dance wit Nikki's cusin.

So now I'm sitting here by myself, drinking on the rest of the Goose that's left. I can feel the liquor kicking in now.

"What's up Face, when you get out?" I hear someone say to my right. Everything starts to spin as I turn and look at the person who's speaking to me.

It's this chick named 'Ashonta,' who I messed around wit a few times back in the day.

"I got out yesterday," I tell her. As we hug one another.

"Who you here wit?" she says.

"A few of my homies. Why what's up?"

"I'm just making sure yo bitch ain't in here, ain't no telling wit yo ass you know you are a ho."

"You got me fucked up! I just pull bitches, dese hos are easy out here fa real," I said.

"I guess nigga!" she says. "You definitely ain't like dat."

"I used to have my way wit you," I say to her.

"Nigga don't get it twisted I just love the way you fuck me," she says.

She sits down and, I ask her what she is drinking. I'm bout to try to bust dis bitch down tonight, fuck it.

"Oh you think you bout to get you some pussy tonight nigga? Buying a bitch a drink and shit."

"Ma chill wit all dat, I'm just feeling yo company."

"Well okay den get me a 'Blue Muthafucka.'" That's a mixed drink of white and blue food coloring liqueurs. "But don't think you're getting some pussy," she says.

I step to the bar to get her drink. I ended up getting Bang another bottle of Pink Moscato, the homies Five, Young, and Black a bottle of Goose, me a beer, and Shonta a Blue Muthafucka.

I stop give them their bottles, then go to the table wit Shonta.

Five yells over the music. "I see you whore!" Talking bout me kicking it wit Shorty that's at the table.

"Here goes your 'Blue Muthafucka' you asked for," I say giving her the drink. I sit down and we're chilling talking over the music. She's bopping to the music, when her song comes on.

"Hum that's my shit, come dance wit me," she says pulling my hand til I'm on my feet and find myself on the dance floor getting it on to the song 'Bad' by Wale ft. Tiara Thomas.

"So what's up you wit me tonight?"

"What I tell you?" she says.

"I'm saying don't play like you ain't on it ma. I can tell you wanna fuck a nigga how you're dancing on me."

"I can feel yo dick getting hard too wit yo nasty ass," she says.

I slide my hand down by her pussy and say, "So this pussy ain't mine tonight I know it's wet as fuck?"

She says, "You get on my nerves man you know I can't resist you dat dick too good."

"We bout to slide den," I say. "You ready?"

"Hum umm, let me tell my people I'm bout to leave wit you."

The song goes off she leaves and walks off to the other side of the club to holla at her people. I get up wit the fellas, and tell them I'm bout to bounce wit this book I co-authored.

"Dat's what's poppin'," Five says. "I'm here wit Bravo, get at me in the A.M."

"I bout to leave wit Foxy," Bang says. "Shoot to the telly you know."

"It's a bet," I tell 'em.

Then outta nowhere we hear a fight break out.

"Yo where the young hittas at?" I said.

"What the fuck?" Bang says, and we all run over to where the commotion is.

"Bitch ass nigga what's up?" I see a dude saying but, I can't make out his face at the moment. But it's definitely Young he's talking shit to.

Black's getting pulled off of this dude named 'Dog' that he just knocked out and was stomping. "Get the fuck off me bruh!" Black says, wrestling wit the bouncer who wasn't tryna let 'em in.

My nigga Bang then hits, the dude Young was getting into it wit. Five den pulls the cannon out, "I'm right here Face," he says. Now I see the niggas they done got into it wit is the nigga 'Chino' and the other fuck nigga named 'Dog,' that I don't fuck wit.

I grab the bouncer, "Yo get the fuck off my lil homie bruh, what the fuck is wrong wit you?" This nigga den let Black go and turned around on me on some tough shit. I punch 'em right in his shit. Five, done slapped him wit the strap. And all his fronts came out. I don't know if it was his strap dat did it or, the punch I served him wit. Because I punched the shit outta that nigga ...

Blocka, blocka, blocka ... It's Black dumping in the club. Niggas are running, bitches are screaming, and I'm telling my niggas, "Let's go. We gotta get the fuck outta here."

We make it outside, Five jumps in wit me. Bang tells us, to meet up at the spot.

"Yo let's go man!" I say. The young hittas, done jumped out of their whip and, are having a shoot-out wit the dudes we were fighting.

So now Bang and Five, hop out and are on the front line wit the homies at war. I'm out of the truck on the side ducked down, when I see the bouncer that I hit in the bar, come out wit his gun about to shoot Five.

I catch 'em from the side, wit all my might and hit him right in the throat. He drops the gun and is trying to catch his breath, as he stumbles backwards. I pick up the gun and see him coming to me in a raging manner. Pow, pow, pow, pow, pow, ...

His body drops like a sack of leaves. I hear, tires screeching, people still screaming and running, my niggas still shooting at them niggas.

"Let's go y'all!" I yell to the team. Finally, everybody runs to their cars and were burning rubber out of the parking lot.

"Where the fuck you get that pistol from bruh?" Five says.

"Shidd, bruh the bouncer you hit wit the iron in the mouth, was tryna sly fox you my nigga. So I took a chance and, hit the muthafucka in his shit instead of watching him put that lead in you bruh. He dropped the gun, I picked it up and finished dat fool."

"Aye bruh call Bang and tell dem niggas to get ducked off for a lil while, til shit calm down." I tell 'em the number.

Ring, ring, ring, ... "Yo Bang," Five says.

CHAPTER 16
VICKY'S SECRET

"Hello baby what's up?" she says.

"What's up ma? Why haven't I heard from you in a few days?" he says.

"I already told you Face was getting out and we're going to have to slow things down," she said.

"I'm saying you were just saying you were done wit the nigga two months ago, now you're all on the nigga's dick when he gets out! So that's why you didn't pick up your phone a lil while ago?" Jay says.

"Jayson you already know I'ma answer when you call but, we're staying together and I'm not gonna disrespect him like that to his face."

"When can I see you again ma?" Jay asks her.

"I don't know right now, but you'll be able to see me when I get some free time."

"Well, what are you doing now is dat nigga gone, cause you have definitely been on the phone for a min?" Jay says.

"Why are you worried bout him, I'm on the phone wit you ain't I?" Vicky states.

"Worried about who dat dude ain't fucking wit me."

'Hum,' Vicky, thinks to herself. 'If you only knew.'

"Well anyways, Jay, I'm bout to get off this line and get dressed. I just got out of the shower, and you're fucking up a bitch's mood talking stupid shit!"

"My fault bae, I ain't mean no harm. I just want you here with me. Instead of you having to go thru that bullshit you've been dealing wit fucking wit that lame ma," Jayson said.

"Jay you know I love this nigga. It's just crazy now cause, somehow you done found yo way into my life."

"Don't worry yourself baby, just know that I'm here for you," Jay tells her.

"I hear you," she says. "I'll talk to you later."

"Maybe you can come down here and see me."

"I'ma call Kimberly and see if she wanna chill tonight, talk to you in a min."

"Okay baby girl, hit me up if you get a chance. And have something on wit easy access if you decide to let me see you tonight," he says.

"Boy you too much, bye Jayson," Vic says.

"But you're loving it tho, aren't you?" Jay asks.

Click ... The line disconnects.

'I don't know what I'ma do wit these two muthfuckas,' Vicky thinks. 'Face, has been in my life for the past five and a half years. We've been thru our share of ups and downs. I can't deny that I'm truly in love wit his ass. But again at the same time, he's then took me thru so much bullshit.

'Then I met this nigga Jay a few months ago. He's everything I want in a man, but he's not Face. He shows me respect, always wants to be around me, makes me feel special, and to be honest I've fallen for him. But he's not a street nigga like my baby.'

"What am I gonna do?" she says out loud.

She lotions her body, puts on her lace panties and bra, then lays back on her bed and dials Kim's number.

"Hello Vicky, what you want bitch? I'm outside, so come open the door ho," Kimberly says.

"Watch yo mouth ho," Vicky tells Kim. Then heads to the door to open it for Kim.

Knock, knock, knock, ... "Hold up damn!" Vicky says.

"Hurry up Vicky you know it's cold out here."

Vicky opens the door ... "Yuh bitch put some clothes on."

Kim says, "Dis my shit I walk around how I want in my shit. What have you got going on in here ho? You got this bitch smelling all lovely, walking round here like you bout to get you some."

"I just might be, Jayson's ass just called tryna get up wit me. He's crying, cause I ain't been talking to him since my daddy got home," Vic says.

"Kev's punk ass just called me an hour ago, talking about him and Jayson tryna fuck wit us," Kim says.

"I know I just talked to Jay. He wants some pussy, but that's dead," Vicky says.

"Bitch go put some clothes on, you know how I am ho."

"Yeah, well yo ass won't be getting none of this, wit yo carpet munching ass."

"Don't nobody want you but Face and Jay's retarded ass. Wit yo dry fucking pussy, all dem miles on dat shit," Kim says.

"Watch yo mouth ho, cause you know if you wasn't fam ya face would be all in my pussy," Vicky said, walking off to go get dress.

'What am I gone wear,' Vicky thinks looking thru her shit. 'Jayson's ass ain't getting none fuck him. But I am bout to have 'em come meet up wit me, and have a drink.'

"Kim call Kev, and tell them to come thru and meet us at the Paradise," Vicky tells Kim.

"Aight ho but, hurry up tho a bitch is ready to move around and smoke something. You got some loud bitch?" Kim says.

"There should be some on the table, I got it from Face before he left.

"Who dropped you off over here ho?" Vicky asks Kim.

"Tat's crazy self," Kim says.

"You still messing wit her bitch?" Vic yells from the room.

"That's my baby, fa real. That girl got a bitch fucked up Vicky," Kim says.

"Y'all nasty ho, I can't fuck wit nobody who's got the same shit between their legs as me. I love dick too much!" Vicky says.

"Slut get dress and get outta mines, all up in my busy."

"What busy muthafucka wit yo gay ass."

"Whateva bitch so what!" Kim said, breaking down the cigar that was on the table.

Kim rolls the weed, calls Kev's thirsty ass, and they make plans to meet up at the Paradise.

"We'll be there in about an hour and 15 mins," says Kev.

"Aight we'll be there by then," Kim tells him, and they hang up.

"Ho you ain't roll up yet?" Vicky says, walking out of the back.

She has her Jordan stilettos on, they're red, blue, gray, and white. Some Denim Curve jeans, a white and red tube shirt on. Wit the words, 'She 2 Cute' written on the front in blue. And a gray lil jacket on.

With a few accessories to top things off.

"Yea bitch, I had to call Kev's ass, you know that nigga wanna talk a bitch's ear off," Kim says, lighting the blunt.

"I don't know why he's still wasting his time wit you. I already would have bounced on your dusty ass," Vic says.

"I know right the nigga ain't even smelled the kitty yet, thirsty as hell doe." They laugh and Kim passes the blunt.

"He might get it tonight doe how I'm feeling," Kim says.

"I definitely ain't got time to be fucking wit Jay's ass all night. My daddy ain't having dat," Vicky tells Kim.

"You are crazy as hell, playing wit fire like you can't get burned or something," Kim says.

They sit there and smoke their blunt, and put some finishing touches on their hair and make-up before locking the house up and getting into Vicky's car going to the Paradise.

"Vicky, Face gone flip out if he catches yo ass out here creeping tonight. You know how da nigga is and I ain't getting in the middle of that shit either," Kim says to Vic.

"I already know where he's at, at that bitch La'Toya's party. He is probably all up in somebody's bitch face, his ass is lucky I don't go blow down on dat shit," Vicky says.

Ring, ring, ring, ... "Turn the music down for me," Vicky says answering her phone. "Hello where ya'll at?" she says.

"We're like ten minutes away from the bar. It's the same spot we chilled at before, right?" Jayson asks.

"Yea slow poke," Vicky tells him. "We just pulled into the parking lot, so I'll see you when you get here."

"Aight baby girl, I'll be dere," Jay says, and they end their call ...

CHAPTER 17

"Yo where the fuck these niggas at?"

"I thought you said he told you to meet him at the spot bruh?" I said to Five.

"Shidd bro he did!" Five says. "Man it's too much going on tonight," he says frustrated.

"We could have all been up in some pussy tonight, dat party was jumping bro," I say.

"Damn let me call this nigga back, real quick."

"Yea do dat," I tell Five looking at my phone at the incoming call ...

"Hello!" I say into the phone. Nobody says anything, I look at the screen to see who it is that called. It's a blocked caller though. "Man who the fuck is this calling me blocked," I yell into the phone. The person hangs up.

"He's not answering," Five says.

"Where the hell are these crazy muthafuckas?" I say, hitting the steering wheel.

I put the car in reverse, and as I'm pulling out of the driveway the young homies pull up and hop out of the car.

"Fuck," yells Young. "They got Bang pulled over man."

Five and I, hop out as Black's opening the door to the spot.

"What the fuck you mean bruh, how in the hell did he get pulled?" I say.

"Face I don't know, all I saw was him in front of us, we passed a cop coming in the other direction. When outta nowhere the pig hits a U-turn and hits his lights!" Young tells me.

"I thought that muthafucka was coming for us," Black says.

"Y'all ain't got no scanner in here?" Five asks.

"Yeah it's right dere turn that bitch up," Black says.

"Dis shit crazy," I say.

"I know Face bruh, I hope they don't take that nigga to jail," Young says.

"It's bond money on deck but still we don't need dat right now."

"Huh bruh," Black says.

"Hold up turn that up what did they just say on the scanner?"

"He's a Black male about 5'5, looks about 160 pounds, he has an outta state ID, the name on it is 'Chad Face,' and his social is 283-84-6113."

"Check him for any warrants, while I search his car for any weapons," the officer says, then the scanner goes back to static.

"Fuck I hope that nigga got rid of that damn gun man," I say out loud.

"That nigga jumped out of his ride wit suzzi ASAP, when we got to the parking lot," Five says.

"Now you know why he goes by 'Bang,'" Black says.

"I see that muthafucka is trained to go," I say.

"I need back-up over here immediately, the suspect just pulled off!"

"I'm on the back streets of Oak and Nevada, hurry I'm losing him!" we hear the officer yell thru the scanner.

"Damn he needs to get away, and ditch that fucking car," I say.

"He still has that gun, in the car I bet. Why else would he go on a fucking chase like dat?" Young protested.

"Dis shit crazy, all this shit that's happening and you've only been out a fucking day and a half, this muthafucka's just starting fa real," Five says.

"Yeah I know I'm not gone sleep tonight," I say to them.

"I'm losing him, he turned onto Youngstown Rd. towards the Chit and Chew Restaurant, then made a quick right onto Pen St.," the officer says.

"Get away bruh, dat fucking choppa carries a life sentence, ain't no telling what's on that shit," Black says.

"You mean how many bodies are on that shit?" Young comments.

"I'm calling his phone but it keeps going to voicemail," Five says.

"Man Bang needs to answer his phone, so I can go swoop 'em up. I know he's hopped out of that fucking car by now," I say.

"He's on foot, he's heading towards a wooded area going behind Ice Cream Zone and Jimmy's Drive Thru," the officer, breathes thru the speaker.

"Keep running my nigga!" Young says.

"Aye look y'all lock this shit up and get a room at a hotel. I'm bout to ride thru that area, and see if I can bump into dis nigga somewhere out dere," I tell him.

"Five post wit the homies, so we won't look suspect while I'm tryna find bruh."

"Aight I'ma keep tryna contact him," Five says.

"Hit me as soon as y'all hear from him and I'ma do the same," I say, and head for the door.

We all hop in our cars, and go in our separate directions.

I get by the Avon Oaks Apts. By where they are looking for Bang and it's cops everywhere.

I pull into the complex, this is where Kim's apartment is, I'm in her parking lot across the street from the Ice Cream Zone.

'They got that fucking place surrounded like he's in the damn building,' I'm thinking. 'Let me try his phone,' I think dialing the number ...

"After the beep please leave a message for Banga ..." Beep!

"Call me back ASAP!" I say and hang up.

I look to my left and I see an old school, pulling from beside a car that looks like my girl's car.

'What the fuck that shit looks like Vicky's whip,' I think. "Man I know she ain't trying me like dat, out this fucking late," I say calling her phone.

It's two dudes in the old school, when they ride past me I don't know who they are I can't see into the car.

"Hello," she says.

"Where the hell are you at" I respond.

I see the gun, from the other situation stuffed in between the console and the driver's seat and I damn near panic. I look up and I see cops heading over to the apartment complex.

"I'm at Kim's," she's saying, but I didn't ever hear it.

"Open the door bae!" I told her so fast and hung up, I grabbed the burner hopped out and hurried to Kim's apartment.

Before I could knock the door was open. I shut the door behind me damn near slamming it.

"Face what's wrong and why have you got that gun?"

"It's a long story bae," I say taking off my shoes.

"Bro you good?" I hear Kim say.

"Yeah I'm straight."

"The police chased my nigga on a high speed chase, he's in this area somewhere he's hopped out of the car," I say, calling his phone again.

It rings this time, but still no answer.

"Why do you have that gun?" Vicky asks me.

"I told you already it's a long story. But why the hell are you over here and not at home?" I ask.

"I told you before you left I might be wit Kimberly tonight. I wasn't bout to be home alone all night while you're out doing who knows."

"Don't try me like dat Vicky. Now what if I would have went straight home, yo ass would have been way over here huh?" I say.

"Chill y'all," Kim says. "I'm bout to lay it down let me know if you leave, so I can lock the door," she says looking at Vicky.

"We chilling it's hot as fuck out dere right now," I tell her.

"Take off yo jacket and come lay wit me," Vicky says, lying on Kim's couch.

I take my jacket off, slide the pistol under the couch and sit down beside her.

"Come here," she says.

"Hold on baby let me text my bro's phone real quick, and let him know to call me ASAP." 'I hope this nigga got away,' I think to myself.

I send the text message, put my phone down and take off my shirt and lay back wit my girl.

"Boo I hope you're not caught up in a mess, you just got home."

"It's nothing bae, don't worry yourself."

"Face I'm serious, please don't get back into the streets."

I hold her and just think to myself, 'It's too late, I'm all in already.'

I'm lying there and I can't sleep so many thoughts are going thru my head. 'Who the fuck were those dudes, in that Chevy? They were looking in my truck like they knew me. I wonder where the hell my nigga is. I pray he got away. How many people got shot tonight? How many families have funerals to attend now?'

"Baby why are you still awake go to sleep," Vicky says as she turns over and kisses me.

"I can't close my eyes, so much happened tonight," I say to her.

She kisses me again, and says she loves me.

"I love you too boo," I say.

Beep ... Her phone beeps and vibrates.

I'm thinking it's Banga messaging me back, so I get up but it's her phone.

"Who the fuck is messaging you this late Victoria?"

"Nobody it's Charmaine," Vicky says. Knowing it's Jay, letting her know he made it home safe.

"What's she been up to, I ain't seen her since I been home?"

"Nothing for real she's been kicking it wit your sister."

"You got a Swisher boo?"

"Yeah why? I thought you weren't smoking."

"Where's the Swisher baby? I can't sleep, so much shit happened tonight I gotta smoke a blunt to calm my nerves."

I get the weed out of my pocket, Vicky grabs a Swisher out of her purse and hands it to me. I roll up the blunt light it, hit it a few times and pass it to Vicky. She hits the L, and passes it back.

"Bae are you okay?" she asks me.

"I don't even know bae, but regardless I'm not going back to jail."
I try to pass her the blunt again, but she declines it this time.

"I'm bout to go to sleep on your ass," Vicky says.

"Go ahead boo, I'm aight."

I'm smoking the rest of the blunt to the face, when I notice my
phone light up about to vibrate from a text message.

"You still up?" It's a message from Nikki.

"Yeah ma, what's up?" I texted back.

"Are you okay, I'm worried about you?"

"I'm good, get some sleep I'ma get wit you when I leave the crib,"
I reply, looking over at Vicky asleep.

I'm high as a muthafucka, I turn on the TV to the five o'clock
news. They're on there talking about the shooting at the club.

"There's been reported two people shot dead unidentified wit
shots to the head," the reported states. "At this moment we have no
suspects in custody. But there are witnesses who may have a lead."

I turn the TV off, and get up. I start pacing back and forth.

I call Five's number ...

"Yo bruh, what's up?" he says, into the phone.

"Aye y'all see the news?"

"Yeah dey ain't got shit right now doe," he says.

"Man look y'all niggas stay ducked off for a while, I'ma chill out
myself for a min."

"Aight my nigga, but what's up wit Bang you hear from him?"

"Naw man but I believe he's aight, I've got a feeling he's cool."

"Call me when you make yo move," Five says.

"I got you bruh y'all niggas don't leave dat room," I say and we
hang up.

I look at the screen and see a text from Nikki.

"Baby be careful, and I hope you know you can always count on
me if you ever need to. Good night!"

"Good night, and I appreciate that baby girl," I texted back.

It's 5:30 a.m., when I finally lie back beside Vicky and fall asleep.

CHAPTER 18

The next morning Vicky's up, her and Kimberly are talking about what they just saw on their Facebook pages, of what happened at the club.

I'm lying there acting like I'm still asleep, but I'm listening to them gossip.

"Damn girl that's terrible, whoever the fuck, did that to them two innocent people," Kim's saying to Vicky.

"I know girl I hope this nigga didn't have anything to do wit dat shit," Vicky says, looking my way.

"On this status it says, something about some lil niggas and that nigga from North Carolina that's been out here."

"The boy who was in yo inbox, about two weeks ago that you said was getting some paper?"

"Yeah that's him," Kim admits.

"Didn't you give him your number?" Vicky asks Kim.

"Yup and I think he tried to reach me at seven o'clock this morning."

'Hold up did she just say my nigga, tried to get at her this morning?' I think, and roll over and see them rolling up.

"What time is it?" I ask.

"Ten til ten," Vicky says, looking at the clock on the wall.

"Turn to the news, real quick," I say, getting up going to piss.

I come out of the bathroom, and there's a picture of Bang on the television screen.

"Girl that's him right there," Kim says.

"Wait right quick y'all let me hear what they're saying," I said.

"Now we have a couple of leads from witnesses leading to this guy, that was on a high speed chase early this morning. He's still out there on the run, officers failed to arrest him, he's considered armed and dangerous.

"WPD says, he was last seen wearing dark blue jeans, a red Bulls jersey, and some black and red shoes.

"Please if you see this man or have any suspicions that could help us catch this man call this number: 1-800-SUSPECT or 330-675-2525, thank you. Over to you now Pam," the reporter says.

I grab my phone, and see a text from Bang.

"Face I'm good, I hope everybody's aight let the team know I'm good and to stay off of the streets for a while."

I call his phone, but still there's no answer.

So I text, "I got you bruh and I'm glad to know you're safe."

He replies, "I'll call you with a new number later bro."

"Aight one," I texted back.

"One," he responds.

I hit Five's number, let them know what's up and told dem that after today get out of that hotel and relocate.

They tell me to bring 'em some smoke when I get a chance, and we end the call.

"Please tell me, you ain't in the middle of all of that shit Face," Vicky says.

"Look bae, let me hit that blunt. I told you it was a long story and I'm not bout to explain it all right now."

"Look what you got yourself into already."

"Bae pass me the blunt and chill yo ass out they don't know shit about me in the middle of nothing," I say.

"Face you ain't been out two days, and you're on dis bullshit bro," Kim says, passing me the blunt.

"I already know," I said shaking my head. "But look tho, I'm bout to bust this move. I gotta get this situation in order."

"Be careful bae," she says.

"I'ma be aight," I say to her.

"I'm serious I don't want you to get hurt or, go back where you came from," says Vicky.

I grab the pistol from under the couch, and can feel the body I just caught all on it.

"I'ma call you in a lil bit babe," I say to Vicky. She hugs me and gives me a kiss. "Mmmwahh!"

"Love you, love you too!" we tell each other.

I put on my jacket, and Kim's saying, "Bro be safe."

"Aight sis, pick up the phone when I call y'all," I tell them, and walk out of the door.

"Fuck I gotta hide this damn truck," I say as I get in and start it up.

I look at the screen on my phone and peep four updates of notifications on my FB page. It's inboxes from Terria, Nikki, and Ashonta ...

Terria, saying she's going to the ATL for a while and she hopes I don't forget about her.

"How could I forget about you beautiful?" I hit her back.

Nikki says, "I'm up thinking of you. I wish you would stop playing with me. Please be safe out there." I don't think she's gotten any sleep, cause she was texting me late as hell ... well early this morning. And this had to come while I was asleep.

"Playing with you how?" I reply.

Ashonta's message says ... "What happened, are you okay Face? Hit me up ASAP," and she leaves her number.

I don't reply, but I dial her number after I log off of my page.

I put the truck in gear, and pull off as Shonta answers her phone.

"Hello," she says, sounding tired.

"You asleep?" I say.

"I was till you woke me up."

"My fault baby girl, hit me up when you wake up ma."

"No you're okay, I gotta be up anyway," she says.

"Sorry our plans got interrupted last night, I saw you were worried about me though."

"It's okay. What happened though you had me scared?"

"It wasn't anything that had to do with me," I lied.

"You don't have to lie to me. Aight? All I wanna know is are you okay?" Shonta says.

"Yea I'm aight ma, but listen what are you doing later?"

"I'ma be moving today, but hit me up we can chill later."

"It's on baby I'll call you later."

"Yup," she says. Then we end our call.

I'm riding down, Southern Blvd. on my way to my aunt's house. I gotta get up wit Rayn to re-up. And I'm gonna park my car over there for a min till this heat cools off.

A.D.'s calling in as I'm turning onto Tod, bout to pass the Warren Village.

"Yea what's poppin' cuz?" I answer.

"Bruh, where you at?!" he says.

"Man what's up bro ...? I'm on my way to my aunt's on da North."

"Lil bruh stay dere I'm pulling up in fifteen mins!" he says, hanging up in my ear.

I bend a few more corners five mins later I pull into my aunt's driveway all the way to the back.

I hope somebody's here, cause their truck is gone.

I'm out of the truck in a heartbeat and knocking on the back door.

"Who dat?" I hear Rayn saying.

"It's Face bro," I say.

He opens the door. "What's up nephew?"

"You already know man, I need dat smoke. But just something to smoke fa real, I'm done trapping dat shit. It's too slow for me man."

"I knew you weren't bout to be fucking wit it long you're a dopeboy fa real," he says.

"You already know unk."

"So what do you want tho man like a quarter?" he says.

"Dat would be cool," I tell him.

He puts it together then says, "Just shoot me eighty."

"You got it," I say giving him the bread.

We're chilling chopping it up for a lil.

"Man shit got real last night unk, I ain't been home three days, and in some bullshit."

"Well you already know to shoot first and ask questions later," he tells me.

Beep, beep, beep, ... It's the horn to A.D.'s car.

"Dat's my ride man, look I'm bout to leave the whip here for a second til shit calm down."

"Aight, remember what I said, always shoot first and ask questions later."

"Yup," I said leaving out of the door.

I adjust the strap on my hip, as I enter into A.D.'s ride.

"Man lil cuz what the hell popped off last night?" A.D. said as I settled into my seat.

"Shidd cuz, I really don't know. But it got turned up I know dat."

"You know, the streets got yo name all in dat shit fam. You can't be pushing da truck for a while," he says.

"I already know man dat shit all on the news and mo' shit bruh," I say.

"Say doe cuz, shoot to the store right quick, so I can grab a pack of Milds and cigarillos."

"Aight, but dam cuz right when I get this mean plug on dat work, you get caught up in some bullshit," he says.

"I just sit back and replay the scene from the night before in my mind."

So we're riding sliding to the store, but I feel an urge to look to my right out the window. And guess who's beside us ... the young homies, pulling into the store making their way thru the drive-thru.

"Yo cuz pull up beside that car right there," I pointed towards the hot ass rental these niggas are in.

"Who dat bruh?"

"That's the muthafuckas this shit popped off over in the first place.

A.D. pulled beside dem. Wit the windows tinted on his ride, they couldn't see who was in his car.

"They can't see us, but I can see, that they're clutching the handles of their pistols scared as hell."

I roll my window down, and notice the relaxation come across their minds from the expressions on their faces.

"Man what da fuck are y'all niggas doing out here? I told y'all to stay put til everything cools down."

"We had to check da spot, we're on our way back to the room now doe my nigga," says Young.

"Where the fuck's Five?" I ask dem.

"When we woke up this morning that nigga was gone," Black says. "He left a note tho, and said he talked to you and that you think Bang is safe, and he also said that you ain't want us to leave the room til shit cools down."

"That nigga Five trippin' man, I told that fool to stay put man. What the fuck man!"

"Face you got some loud on you bruh?" Young asks.

"Yea lil bruh, we bout to pull in a parking spot. When y'all get done at the window pull up on me."

"Dem young niggas looked like dey were bout to smoke something cuz," A.D. said.

"Dey bout that life bruh, I caught 'em in action. Shit got ugly wit dem lil niggas quick," I said.

They park beside us, and Black hops in wit me and A.D. "Shit bruh let us get a lil eighty right quick," he says.

"I got y'all dis on me, but look I need y'all to dump this strap in the Mahoning River for me doe," I said to Black.

"Say no more bruh, it's done," the lil homie tells me.

I pass him the pistol and the smoke. We peace each other up and he hops back in the car wit Young.

Young hits the horn, as I salute him then pull off.

'Dem some real young niggas,' I think, as I told A.D. to hold up while I run inside the store to get the Milds and cigarillos.

"Grab me a deuce-deuce cuz," he tells me.

I am walking back to the car, when I see an old school Chevy that looks like the one I saw leaving Kim's parking lot. "Who the fuck, was in the car last night?" I say to myself opening the door, getting into the passenger seat.

CHAPTER 19

We're back in traffic, riding thru town when cuz hit the music turning it down, and says ... "Cuz you was listening to me when I said I got a plug for us right?"

"What about it fam?" I say, thinking how slow this weed shit been going fa real.

A.D. says, "The nigga got dat loud by the tons. But he also has the dog food for cheap."

"I really ain't into this loud shit cuz, it's too slow for me. What's the ticket on dat food doe bruh?"

"I can hit 'em up and see. But who have you got that can get it off like dat?" A.D. asks.

"I'ma get it off," I tell 'em ... But I'm really hoping Strong can let me get down wit him to move it.

A.D. takes a drink of his deuce-deuce and says he'll hit 'em up and see what he can do.

My phone rings ... It's Five calling me.

"Hello man where the hell are you at bruh?" I say.

"I'm wit Junie, this nigga has a sweet lick for us bruh."

"Five shit crazy out here man, and you're talking bout a lick. Do you know our names are all over the streets right now bruh?" I said to him.

"I know big bruh, but shit real. I gotta eat ain't nothing free out here my nigga."

"I respect that you gotta get yours, but dog you gotta remember that shit just hit the fan out here."

"All is well bruh, I'ma get wit you after I bust dis jugh," Five says.

"Mighty lil bruh, hit me when you make dat happen. Be safe too man."

He hangs up and I look at A.D. "What's up what's on your mind nigga?" A.D. says.

"It's lil bruh this nigga bout to make a jugh, right but, we are already hot as hell and I ain't feeling my nigga busting dat move right now. Ya dig?"

"He gotta eat Face dat's just like when you were out dere cuz."

"Dat's why I'm not knocking what he's tryna do," I say to A.D., remembering those nights when I had to put in that work bare-faced with no mask.

The music's back playing and we're bobbing our heads to the beat, but I just keep seeing the way the bouncer's body dropped the night before. And how my niggas were holding it down under pressure. That shit was crazy man, I can only imagine how those mothers feel having to bury their sons and not knowing who's responsible for the madness behind it all.

"Aye cuz whose house is this?" I ask seeing us pulling up in front of a nice white house.

"Come on cuz," says A.D. turning the car off after parking on the side of the street close to the curb.

There are cars parked in the driveway and it looks like the house is full of people.

We step out of the car and proceed to the door.

"Man I hope it ain't a house packed wit a bunch of muthafuckas," I say.

"You scared bruh, dat shit got you in shock from last night?"

"Nah but, shit bro whose crib is dis man? If it ain't no ho's I ain't tryna kick it."

A.D. knocks on the door, and says, "You should know by now cuz all I do is fuck wit bitches. Dese niggas will get you locked up round dis bitch."

"Who is it?" a female's voice sounds behind the door.

"Open the door you know who it is!" A.D. responds.

"Muthafucka you better lower yo tone coming over here demanding shit!" the beautiful goddess says, as she opens the door.

A.D., smiles at her feistiness. "You're turned up today huh, cause you got yo people in here?" he says, stepping inside with me trailing behind.

"Lea this is my cuzin Face, Face this is Lea and her people," he says, introducing me to his girl and her fam.

"What's up, how are y'all doing?" I speak, looking around at the lovely ladies in my presence.

"We know yo cuzin," Lea says, to A.D.

"Umm hmm sure do," says a familiar face, coming around the corner from the kitchen. "It's been a min since I've seen you nigga, hope you still ain't scared of dis pussy," she says, flossing in front of her friends tryna claim a nigga fa real.

"Scared Tesha, calm down I ain't never been scared of no pussy," I speak up.

"So what happened to you that night we made plans?"

"Not nothing fa real, you know shit happens fa real." Really though I went home to my girl but I'm not gonna tell her.

So everyone speaks and we're all chilling, I done rolled up outta my smoke sack I copped earlier.

A.D. and Lea's chopping it, Tesha and I are rapping wit one another. The kush is burning slowly, and it's got me outta my mind.

"Where's the bathroom?" I ask.

"Go down the hall in the back and it's two doors down on the left," Lea says.

I make it to the bathroom and shut the door behind me. I finish pissing and flush the toilet, when someone knocks on the door and turns the knob and steps in closing the door behind dem.

I'm zipping my pants up, when Tesha grabs my hand and turns me around til my back is pressed against the bathroom door.

She unzips my pants and kneels down, pulling my dick out and jerking it off til I'm semi-hard. I wanna tell her to chill and let's just leave and go somewhere and do us, but with me being fresh out I just go wit the flow.

"Baby calm down why are you so tense? Relax and let me bless you wit the best," says Tesha, then she puts my dick in her mouth causing my head to fall back wit my eyes rolling in the back of my head.

"Fuck ma dis shit is fire," I say in a low voice, gripping her head palming it with a nice rhythm while she deep-throats me.

She comes up slowly and says, "Bet yo girl ain't sucking this dick like dis." Then she slaps it on her tongue and lips and puts it back into her mouth.

"Damn I'm bout to cum Tesha, suck the dick and let me nut on yo face ma," I say wit my head tilted back, loving this blessing I'm receiving.

"Oh shit my shit is bout to bust ..."

"Come on daddy bust dat nut," she says.

"Oh shit fuck I'm busting baby, let me nut on yo face ma."

"Un un," she says jacking me off catching all of my cum.

"Well swallow all of dis shit den," I tell her pushing her head down causing her to deep-throat me.

She comes back up slowly again catching every last bite of nut inside me. "Mmwahh! All done," she tells me, kissing my dick and getting up off of her knees.

"Damn baby I know these muthafuckas are wondering where we are," I say to her fixing myself.

She's rinsing out her mouth, and looking in the mirror trying to straighten her hair a lil.

Knock, knock, ... "What the hell y'all doing in my bathroom?" Lea says.

"Nothing girl here we come," Tesha says. "You ready?" Tesha says to me.

"Yea let's ride shawty," I say thinking like, 'Damn this bitch is a freak.'

We open the door, and Lea's standing there wit her eyes locked dead on her homegirl.

"Bitch you better not have been fucking in my shit!"

"Bitch ain't nobody been fucking I got my own shit for dat."

As they're talking my phone rings and I answer it and walk right past Lea to the living room.

It wasn't nobody but Vicky asking me if I am okay and, telling me that she loves me.

I sit down on the couch, and everyone's looking at me like I must have a guilty look on my face. "What's up why is everybody all in my grill?" I say.

"Cause nigga you nasty," Lea's sister says getting up to walk outside to her car to get something.

"What where did dat come from?"

"Like you don't know already," she mentions walking out the door.

"Come on cuz we're bout to pull out," A.D. says.

Lea and Tesha, walks back into the living room.

We say bye to everyone, Tesha hugs me and tells me to get at her later, and that I know how to reach her.

A.D. says, "Cuz Lea's sister was trying to get at you."

"Word bro. I ain't know shorty was gone be here so it's not like it's my fault."

"Bruh I ain't even know you knew Tesha," A.D. says.

"That's a long story my nigga," I tell him. As we step outside.

"Aye cuz," A.D. says tilting his head in Lea's sister's direction. Then walking to his ride.

I look over to her and she's sitting in her car on her phone.

I approach her and she looks at me and rolls her eyes.

"Let me call you back," she says to whoever is on her line. Then hangs up on 'em.

"What's up shawty what's the attitude about wit you?"

"Nigga you're all over here caking it wit this bitch and A.D. knew I was over here tryna see bout you."

"Hold up baby girl, that was by accident fa real me and shawty ain't rocking like dat."

"Why were you in the bathroom wit dat bitch den?"

"Shorty walked in on me ma, it was nothing planned or nothing like dat. But hold up before we even get dere to dat. My bad for the inconvenience I ain't know none of this was gone go down like dis, but I would like to get to know you though if that's still open for discussion," I say to her.

"Well I mean if you're not into games and tryna play both parties then we can talk."

"I got you, but look my cuz is bout to pull out, right? So what's yo number so I can get to know you?"

She gives me the number, and steps out to go back into the house. We hug and go our separate ways.

"Damn," I say to myself, when I see all that ass she got behind her. And that's what I save her name as in my mobile, 'Big Booty.'

CHAPTER 20

"Yo shawty what's up, why are you just getting at me," Jay's saying into his phone. "I know you saw my message," he says.

"First nigga I was asleep it was late as hell when you texted me, and second you already know I have a man who just got out!" Vicky explains.

"It's seven o'clock in the evening, you've been with that nigga all day yo? Da nigga ain't letting you breathe or something?" he's saying tryna be humorous but, really is getting on Vicky's nerves.

"I'ma tell you straight like dis Jay, please get to the point of why you keep questioning me bout this nigga. Do you think I'ma bout to quit kicking it wit you or something?

"And to answer your question, no I have not been wit him all day. And he definitely lets me breathe or I wouldn't have been wit you last night."

"You said do I think you're bout to quit kicking it wit me? Why would I feel like dat, dat nigga broke he just got out what can he do for you?"

"You're really sounding like a hater right now Jay, you know dat?" Vicky tells him, getting upset a lil.

"But guess what I don't give a fuck if he is broke and couldn't help me pay my bills, I would still be down for him. And you would still be da one on the side paying for dis pussy nigga!"

Jay can feel their convo turning for the worst, so he trys to clean things up wit Vicky.

"Calm down boo, I ain't mean to rub you the wrong way. What have you got going on later?"

"Why?" she answers.

"I'm tryna get up wit you," he tells her.

"Jay I really don't know about it tonight, I think I'ma stay in the house."

"You can drive out here and stay with me for the night," he says. Taking a sip out of the bottle of Hennessey he is drinking.

"The roads are bad, and I seriously doubt that I wanna be around you right now wit the mood I'm in.

"Maybe when you can talk to me, about us and be worried about us, then I'll come out there and be wit you for the night," she says.

"I am worried about us, why would I have you at my shows when I'm performing when I know it's mad bitches there if I wasn't worried about you?"

"Shows nigga, you really think I give a fuck about a show Jay?!" she shouts. "What the fuck else have you done for me besides fucked me and took me to one of your lame ass concerts?!"

"What!" Jay explodes. "Muthafucka I've done a lot for your phony ass while yo fucking nigga has been locked up, paying bills, buying you shit, making sure there's gas in yo car, what the hell else do I need to say. Huh?"

"You know what, bye Jay! You can scream that shit in the next bitch's ear," Vicky says.

"Oh you don't wanna hear dat shit, yeah I know. I bet that was the nigga's truck in yo people's parking lot I saw when I was leaving," he says.

Click ... Victoria, hangs up the phone on him. "You can tell that shit to the dial tone, cause I ain't the one nigga," she says, getting off her couch heading to the kitchen to get a blunt off of the table.

'I don't know what the fuck got into that muthafucka,' she thinks to herself sitting back down rolling her blunt.

Pissed off she starts to talk to herself, knowing what Jay just said to her has its truth in the matter.

"How in the hell is he gone come at me like dat, he don't know shit bout my man. And so the fuck what you know he's hurting right now, we gone be straight Face always comes thru when it counts," Vicky says to herself.

The weed has her throat dried out, so she gets up to get something to drink.

After grabbing a glass out of the cabinet, she goes to the sink to rinse out her cup to find out that the water has been cut off.

"What the fuck these bitches den came and turned my shit off, I just moved into the muthafucka. And my shit gets turned off," she says hitting the sink with her hand.

'How am I supposed to pay this bill?' Vicky thinks.

"I know Face, is gonna complain if I tell him I need the money to pay it, he just gave me the money for the TV, and on top of that I sold his gun."

"Either Face is going to give it to me, or I'll just go stroke Jay's ego and work his tricking ass outta some money."

She looks in the refrigerator and fills her cup with some juice and goes back to the living room to finish her facial she's smoking.

Picking up her phone she calls Kim to tell her, that the water company came and turned the water off and about Jay's punk ass calling getting on her nerves.

"Hello," Kim says awakened outta her sleep by the phone call.

"Girl, I know yo ass is not still asleep!" Vicky says.

"Bitch are you high, cause you gotta be calling yelling in my ear about me being asleep," Kim says.

"Shut the hell up and listen bitch. Let me tell you bout Jay's ho ass, this nigga calls me right?"

"Okay bitch you're sucking his dick of course he's gone be calling you," Kim says.

"No you stupid bitch listen, this nigga calls me talking shit bout why I didn't message him back last night. Girl you know I had to put the nigga in line ASAP nigga got me fucked up.

"So when I say like, 'Jay you know I got a nigga that just got out,' his lame ass gets in his body, saying shit like my nigga broke he can't do nothing for me. And this and that bullshit," she says.

"Girl I know you went in on his ass," Kim says tuning into the convo and sitting up in her bed.

"Yeah I told him it doesn't matter if Face is broke or not I'm still riding for him. And you gone be the one still paying for this pussy."

"Vicky, something is wrong wit yo ass."

"Dat ain't it though, after that the nigga gone ask me to come out there tonight."

"For what?" Kim says.

"You know what that nigga wants, the same thing Kev's muthafucking ass be feining for from you."

"Speaking of Kev, this is him breaking in now. Let me call you back in a min," Kim says ending their call.

"Aight bitch call me back, and get yo ass up and get dressed."

"Bye ho," Kim says.

Vicky is sitting there high as ever, when Face and A.D. walk into the house.

"Hey bae what's up?" Face says to his woman.

"Nothing where have you been Face?" she says.

"Fa real, nowhere just fucking wit this nigga all day."

"What's up Vicky?" A.D. speaks.

"Hi," she says. "Hope you ain't had him around no hos, knowing you y'all was around some bitches."

A.D.'s laughing it off, says, "Nah man cuz ain't fucking wit shit anyway."

"Umm, get the hell outta here. Who do you think I am?" she says, getting up off of the couch going to the back to their room.

"Damn cuz I see why you wit her," A.D. says, nodding his head in Vicky's direction.

I look in her direction, and say, "Yeah she's fat back dere a lil cuz." Talking bout her ass.

"But, real shit she's crazy doe man," I tell him.

"Face, come here for a min," Vicky yells from the room.

"What's up bae?" I say, entering the room.

"The water company came and turned the water off," she says.

"What the fuck, made them do that?"

"I don't know, cuz I know I'm paid up on my bills."

"Call 'em and see what's going on and let me know what's up," I tell her.

"You eat?" she asks me.

"Yeah I had a lil something."

"Okay well I'm gonna call now and see what's going on wit this water situation."

"Aight, well let me know boo. I'm bout to go re-up this dumb ass weed shit is too slow for me."

"Be careful bae," she says.

"Aight talk to you later."

"I'm gonna be wit Kimberly, cuz I ain't staying in here all day."

"Dat's cool, bae," I say walking out of the room.

'Damn if it ain't one thing it's another,' I think walking into the living room where A.D. is on the phone.

"Yeah what's the ticket again on that food bruh?" A.D. is saying to whoever he's talking to.

"Dat's cool man, I'm bout to be over there to see what it's looking like."

"Cool one," A.D. says, then hangs up.

"What's up cuz, what is dude talking?" I ask him.

"The ticket is sweet cuz, the nigga only wants seventy dollars a gram."

"Word dat's cool bruh, let's go see the product," I say.

"Baby I'm bout to slide. Call me when you get to Kim's," I tell Vicky as she comes back into the living room.

"Okay daddy," she says kissing me on the lips.

"Love you and be careful."

"I will, love you too."

"It's on Vicky," A.D. tells her.

"Bye Amp, and don't have him around any hos.

"Lock the door," she says then goes to the back to get some clothes to take to Kim's. Knowing that she is not coming back here tonight.

"Where do we gotta go to look at this shit cuz?" I say.

"Back to the East over there, where 'Worm (RIP)' and 'Tino' is," A.D. says.

"Where at Claney's?"

"Yeah," he says. "I think they're bout to buy that bar too,"

"Damn, dey letting you get it for seventy dollars a gee bro?"

"Dem niggas are out here eating Face."

"I been hearing bout it, dey been telling me to fuck wit 'em for a min too."

"I'm telling you lil bruh dey got it man," A.D. says.

"Well let's go see what's up, what are you waiting on cuz?"

A.D.'s reversing out of my driveway, as I get a text message from Shonta. Saying, 'Bring a bottle wit you when you come over.'

"It's a bet, I got you," I reply back.

CHAPTER 21

We're turning into Claney's parking lot, across from the I.G.A. grocery store and liquor store across the street.

"Aye bruh when we leave here, pull over there to the liquor store so I can get a bottle," I say to A.D.

There's two bad bitches walking outta Claney's, as I'm shutting the passenger door to A.D.'s car.

"What's up Amp?" the taller one of the two says.

"What's up wit y'all?" he says back.

"Hey A.D.," the other one of the pair says.

"Ughhh, Face you can't speak?" she says.

"Oh what's up ma, I was zoned out for a min."

"I can see," she says. "You can bring your eyes back up and stop roaming."

"My bad but you're just so beautiful, I just had to examine every inch of you."

A.D. continues inside to see the work, and what it's going for.

"Cut it out," she tells me blushing from my comment.

"So where do you know me from, how do you know my name?" I asked.

"You serious?" she says, looking like I just insulted her.

"Now that we're rapping your face looks, familiar but I can't put a name wit it right now."

She shakes her head and says, "I'm the one that brought you, your ID when you lost it the day of that high speed chase."

"That's you I'm sorry about that ma, I don't know how I can forget a face like this."

Her friend's in the car, and she's looking like she's ready to leave.

She smiles, and says, "My homegirl's tryna make it somewhere on time it was nice seeing you."

"Hold up ma, take my number." I give her the number and tell her to get at me.

"We'll see, by the way what's my name?" she says.

Everything goes blank in my mind when she says that to me.

"Strike one," she tells me, walking off getting into the car with her friend.

"Nigga come on man out here stuck on dem hos," A.D. says, coming out of the front door to Claney's to get me so I can go in with him to see the work.

We slide in and, Worm motions for us to follow him to the back.

He tells some lady working the bar to get us triple shots of whatever we want on the house.

I fuck with the white so I tell her to bring me some Goose, A.D. likes the dark liquor so he says he'd prefer Hennessey, but he'll take whatever they have brown.

"What's up lil bruh you just now making it out?" Worm says to me.

"Yeah man dem few months broke a nigga down too, but it helped me mentally."

"We all go thru stuff we gotta know how to stay focused and overcome the situations," he says pulling out an ounce of heroin and an ounce of white powdered substance.

"Here are your drinks," the bartender says handing the drinks to us.

"Thanks," I say to her. A.D. tells her thanks as well.

"Y'all welcome," she tells us. Walking out to continue her work.

Worm, pulls back out the drugs from his desk drawer as his employee leaves the room.

"What did you say the ticket was again?" A.D.'s asking him.

"I told ya seventy a gee, but this shit is better then the other shit I had. So it's going for ninety a gee nephew," Worm tells A.D. passing him the dog food.

I haven't ever really messed with heroin at the time, so I'm just sitting staring at it for a second while A.D. examines the product.

"What do you want for the powder?" I ask, breaking the trance I was in thinking about the H.

"You can get this at a stack an ounce," he says tossing the work to me.

I take a sip of my drink and tell him I'll take it. A.D. tells, him he wants the dog food. So after cashing out for the drugs, we're sitting talking for a min finishing the drinks.

My phone rings ...

"Yoooo," I say into the receiver.

"Where are you, come get me whore," Five tells me.

"I'm East bound lil bruh, where are you nigga?" I say.

"On the East too nigga, come scoop me. I'ma be at 'Smart Mart' in 2 mins bro."

"Aight nigga I'm wit A.D. we're bout to pull up. You bust that move with the lick?"

"Yeah nigga come get me!" he says, I can hear it in his voice and breathing that his heart is pumping fast from the adrenaline rush.

"Stay dere man we're on our way."

"Let's ride bruh we gotta get Five, dat nigga done bust dat move," I tell A.D.

"Y'all niggas be careful wit dat work and get at me," Worm's saying this as we're hurrying to the car.

"Shoot down to Smart Mart that's where he is." That's what I tell A.D., but my mind is on the powder that I just got.

"Where the fuck is he?" A.D. says, as we're pulling into the lot.

"Da nigga said he was up here man hold up for a min."

"Dere he is," I say to A.D. He sees him and pulls up on 'em.

"Come on bruh," A.D. yells to Five out of the window.

"Bro go back up to the liquor store, before we go fuck wit dis shit," I say referring to the drugs we have on us.

"Man that nigga Junie is wild as fuck," Five says, pulling a Black and Mild out of his pocket beginning to freak it.

"Why do you say dat?" I ask.

"The muthafucka kicked out this nigga's window to his car, and finds a safe in the back seat with some H, in it and some bread."

"How did he know there was a safe in the car?"

"I don't know, but guess what happened man ...? The nigga came out of the house, as we're getting the safe out from the back seat, and starts popping off at the mouth. I can't get to my ratchet in time to shut the nigga up cause I got the safe in my hands. So this nigga Junie, runs up on the dude and puts his burner in the dude's face backing him back into the house."

"Man y'all did this in broad day?" I ask.

"Bruh it is what it is, but look I'm nervous as a bitch cause people are driving past looking crazy."

"So what happened bro?" A.D. said.

"Shit I take the lil safe in the house, and see Junie wit the burner in dis nigga's mouth, he's got tears coming down his face scared as hell."

A.D. parks in 'Diddy's' parking lot. I run in and grab the bottle and more blunts.

When I come back Five's finished wit the story.

"Aye bruh, let's go to the crib and put this dope up."

"Aight," A.D. says getting back in traffic.

I'm busting the blunt open, so I can empty the guts out and put the kush inside.

"Face what did you do wit dat pistol from last night?" Five asks me.

"I got rid of it nigga what the fuck you thought I was gon keep it? A muthafucka just got hit wit that bitch you already know I ain't bout to keep it."

"I was just making sure you don't still have it dat's all fool."

We're pulling in to A.D.'s house, when my cell rings.

"Who the fuck is this?" I say looking at the screen.

"Who dis?" I say answering the call.

"It's Banga bro, what's popping everybody aight?"

"Bro what's good, where are you?"

"Man I'm on the highway heading back to N.C., but check dis my nigga I got shit stashed in da garage at the spot. Go grab it for me it's in a black trash bag inside the garbage can right by the grill."

"What do you want me to do wit it doe my nigga?"

"Get rid of it bruh, and da bread dat's with it, send it in the morning wit the young homies. Tell dem niggas I said to get back dis way ASAP."

"Don't trip bruh I got you, just make it there safe and call me when you reach yo destination."

"It's on my nigga," Bang says.

"One bruh," I say, praying he has a safe drive.

After ending the call, I step out of the car leaving the bottle I have in the car. Placing the L I just rolled behind my ear I twist the door knob to the house and enter.

"Face, dis shit strong as a bitch," A.D. says talking about the dope he just copped.

"I can smell it from here," I said. Walking into the kitchen covering my nostrils wit my hand.

I'm thinkin' bout what Bang was just saying to me on the phone, wondering what's in the bag I don't hear Five saying, "Bruh ya phone is ringing."

"Good looking I ain't even hear this muthfucka bruh," I told Five answering the phone.

"What's good Shawty?"

"When are you coming here nigga?" Shonta says.

"I'm bout to be on my way in 2.2 baby girl."

"You got the bottle already?"

"Most definitely."

"Aight come on ugly," she tells me.

"Yup give me a min ma," I say.

"Yo Five you tryna slide wit me, to fuck wit dese bitches and drink dis bottle?" Asking him after ending the call wit her.

"You already know man," he says, pulling some bread out of his pocket counting it.

"You gon drop us off bruh?" I ask A.D., watching him place a substance on the table to cut the H with.

"I got y'all, let me get this shit together right quick," he said, studying the work.

"I might as well whip dis shit up den," I say pulling the powdered cocaine outta my jacket.

"You ain't waste no time getting back to it," Five mentions. Lighting the Black back up from where it went out.

"Naw bro, I just couldn't do it weed ain't my thing."

"Here man light this up and put that out," I say to Five handing him the blunt.

"Hell yeah," he said, grabbing the L and putting the Mild out.

"Aye man, where's the shit so I can whip dis up dukes?" I say to A.D.

"Face it ain't been dat long since you've been gone you know where I keep everything," he told me focusing on the task at hand.

"You expect me to know where everything is at in the muthafucka. Huh?"

Rummaging thru the cabinet I find the small Pyrexs. Turning on the oven placing a pot wit water in it over the eye. I pass Five back the blunt, and drop the ounce of cocaine into the Pyrex and add a lil water. Putting the Pyrex into the pot, I watch the dope start to sizzle a bit.

"Aye bruh, pass me that butter knife."

I'm whipping the work when lil bruh says, "Face you ain't put no baking soda in dat shit?"

"Nigga dis dat straight drop shit you don't know nothing bout dog."

"You got me fucked up, I used to watch my pops whip bricks."

"Yeah aight, turn on that cold water for me," I tell him, noticing the dope is ready for its locking process.

With the L in the corner of my lips I'm bringing the girl back to a cookie.

"Here nigga take this blunt," I say to Five. I grab the newspaper, placing the Pyrex on it upside down and hitting the bottom dropping the whole slab out breaking it into pieces.

"Cuz you bout ready?" A.D. says, coming over and seeing the slab on the newspaper on the counter top.

"I'm wrapping dis shit up now bruh," I say, finishing up wit da work.

"I see you still got yo touch wit dat shit."

"Dis right here is nothing, I used to whip 'em up by the nine. Before dem niggas from outta town robbed me and the homies last year, when we went to cop a few birds."

"If I was around when dat went down, I definitely would have caught me a body dat day," Five says, passing the blunt back to me.

"Dat shit ain't nothing we bout to be eating real soon," I say bagging the ounce up, thinking about what Bang had just told me bout not too long ago.

Coughing on the L, Five says, "Yo who are dese bitches we're bout to go fuck wit?"

"Shorty from the bar last night who I was chopping it with, her people will be over dere too so you might find a book to read."

"I hope so cause I really ain't tryna fuck wit my chick in the Hamps tonight," he tells me lighting his Mild.

I finish with what I was doing, A.D. goes and stashes the heroin he just packaged up.

Coming back into the kitchen, he says, "Y'all niggas ready cause after I drop y'all off I gotta go let someone test dis shit." Putting the lil tester he brought back into his jacket pocket.

"Let's ride bruh," I say.

"You want this Mild Face?" Five asks me.

"I'm good right now."

"Let me hit dat shit," A.D. tells lil bruh.

"Nigga when did you start smoking Milds?" Five says, passing the Black.

"Been smoking 'em, just not every day like y'all young niggas."

105

I'm grabbing, my jacket and hat, thinking like, 'Damn I hope the damn water company made a mistake and Victoria don't need no bread,' right?

After getting back in A.D.'s whip he says, "So where does dis broad stay cuz?"

"Fa real fa real, I don't even know let's hit her up and see. I know earlier she said something bout moving today," I say to A.D. dialing her number.

CHAPTER 22

"Aight I'm bout to pull up on you in a few minutes ma," I say, ending the call with Shonta.

"Yo cuz slide to the West Side by where my moms stays."

Riding thru the city to Shonta's house, A.D.'s on his phone telling his junkie that he's bout to pull up in a second. Five's bobbing his head to the music.

And I'm just in the zone, thinking bout my life, and what's all happened in these past couple of days.

"Make a left here cuz," I tell A.D. As we pull up to the stop sign on 6th Street and Deerfield in view of my mom's house.

Sliding down my old street I was raised on, brought back memories of when life didn't have this many challenges. Everything always seemed right back then, my mom was always happy and in a good mood. But now ever since I've been an adult it's not that simple any more.

"I miss the good days ..." I say out loud.

"What?" A.D. said.

"Nothing bro make a right here, I was just trippin' bout something."

"You good my nigga?"

"Yeah, stop right here dat's shawty right dere."

"Dat's the chick from the bar," Five says.

"Yup lil bruh," I respond.

"My nigga fa real, I think my pops has got a lil girl by shawty."

"Word bruh?" I said, as we're getting out of the car.

"Hell dat's her too my nigga."

"Shit's crazy as hell nowadays bruh," I say, grabbing the bottle I brought off of the seat.

"Y'all hit me up later," A.D. tells us.

"Aight one love," I say.

"Yup be careful," he says pulling away as I close the door.

I see the U-Haul has been damn near finished with, as I walk past it to the front door.

"Bout time you made it over here," Ashonta addresses me.

"Fall back baby I told you I was coming thru," I say.

"Here help me wit this box."

"Take this bottle right quick, I got the box for you."

"Jamal what's up? Don't stand and look like you don't know me nigga," Shonta says to Five, calling out his first name.

"What's up?" Five speaks to her.

"Shit nigga you can grab something too, while you're just standing dere."

"Dis box is light as hell," I said, lifting the box.

"It was heavy for me, I hurt my back putting it in here," she says.

"You sure dat's what hurt yo back?"

"Shut up ... Hell yeah that's what hurt my back I ain't been doing nothing."

"How long has it been?" I ask her.

"It's been a min," she tells me.

"Yeah okay, hold the scream door right quick."

I walk the box inside and sit it down in the living room.

"Hi Face!" everyone says, except the oldest sister Sha'Kira. By the look on her face I can see that she is wondering why I'm here and who I'm here for, as she walks out the door.

"What's good wit y'all?" I say.

"Face bring that box back here," Shonta tells me leading me to her room.

We make it to her room. "Looks like she's mad," Shonta says.

"Shit I don't know what for," I say.

"Nigga you know."

"It ain't like she's been riding with me when I was just in the County. Or like she didn't know you and I messed around before."

"I don't give a fuck anyway, I had you first," Shonta said, as we walked back into the living room.

I made my way back outside, leaving Five and the rest of them in the house.

Getting to the U-Haul, I see Sha'Kira. She's moving some stuff around.

"Do you need me to help you with that?" I ask hopping into the back of the U-Haul with her.

"No!" Kira says, pulling out a pack of Newports and lighting one.

"Is that everything?!" Shonta, peeps her head out the screen door and yells.

"Yeah!" Kira, yells back with attitude.

"Bitch don't be mad at me," Shonta comments knowing Kira's salty because Face is over here but not, for her.

"Whatever ho I'm not even bout to go there wit you," Kira mumbles, under her breath to where only I can hear.

"Sha'Kira what's wrong wit you. Why do you got an attitude?" I say to her, getting her attention for a moment.

"I don't have an attitude and there's nothing wrong wit me."

"So can I have a hug then?"

"No," she says. Continuing moving stuff around in the truck straightening it out.

"Why?" I said, trying to pull her close to me.

"Cause I said no," she tells me pulling herself free from me.

"Can I hit your cigarette?"

"Nope ..."

"Damn can I have one den?"

"No get one from that bitch, you called her and you're over here for her right?"

"I ain't know yo number by heart, you changed yo number when I was in the County."

"So you called my sister nigga?"

"I just remembered her number but fa real, I've been wanting to get up with you since I've been out so we can talk."

"We don't have shit to talk about go talk to that bitch, dat's who you came over here for."

"Yo why are you on this bullshit, you're the one who dipped out on me fa real?"

"Just move out of my way so I can go take this U-Haul back," she says.

"I'm coming wit you," I said, really wanting her to say come on.

"No the hell you're not," she says hopping out of the back of the truck and telling me to get out.

"What's yo new number then, can I at least call you?"

"Don't worry about it, call Shonta's trifling ass."

'Damn shawty is really on some fuck me type shit right now,' I'm thinking, but fuck it tho I'm thru wit dis bird. So I guess I can say that's the end of that book.

"Why are you on that bullshit?" I'm asking her as she gets in the U-Haul starting it up.

"Nigga fuck up," she says, behind the window pulling off.

Going back inside where everyone is, they're all looking at me with these stupid faces. I sit down next to Five on the couch and tell him what happened with Kira.

Five says, "Bro fuck dat bitch my nigga, you and Vicky are rocking right now anyway. And we got these hos in here too."

"I wasn't sweating that shit my nigga, it was just crazy how she was salty doe. You feel me?"

"Yeah bro."

"What are ya'll over dere whispering about?" Shonta says.

"I know," says one of her sisters.

"Nothing fa real, just chopping it bout some shit that happened earlier today."

"Yeah right, but shidd doe open dat bottle," Shonta says.

"Go ahead and open it," I tell her.

"Y'all got some smoke?" Shay asks.

"Yup."

"Shit nigga roll up," Saddies said.

"Five twist dis up right quick," I said giving him the loud and the cigarillos.

So we're all chilling everybody's getting their buzz on. Shonta comes and sits by me, my nigga Five is chopping it wit Saddies on the other couch. I'm on my phone on my Facebook page posting a status.

"Take a shot wit me," Shonta tells me.

"You know I really ain't a drinker like dat, but I got you."

"You scared to drink wit me?"

"Naw, but I see what you're on doe."

"What's dat mean?"

"You're tryna get me fucked up ..."

I take a shot wit her, and as time passes I find myself knocking shots down wit her back to back.

"What time is it?" I ask. Not to anyone in particular.

"Bro it's a lil after ten o'clock," Five lets me know.

"Man I'm over here fucked up, messing wit y'all," I say to Five.

"I'm feeling aight too on a real."

"Huh bruh ..."

"I'm about to slide to my people's crib across the street. And crash over dere til morning bruh," Five says.

"Who stays over dere my nigga?" I ask.

"My aunt ..."

"It's a bet, den bruh. Make sure you get at me in da A.M. There's something we gotta take care of."

"Aight, my nigga," he says as we share a brotherly dap/hug.

Shonta walks into the back, I hear her telling her kids to lay down that it's time to go to bed.

Her sisters are chilling too on their phones.

And I'm thinking about Vicky, contemplating either calling her to come get me or having Shonta take me to the crib. I also have to bust that move with what Bang told me about.

I remember to call the young homies, Black and Young. To let them know to meet me at the spot in the A.M., so we can do what we need to do and get that paper en route to Bang. Ring, ring, ring, ...

"Hello ..." Young answers.

"Yo what's good my nigga?" I say.

"Shit man ready to leave this room, we've been cooped up in it all day."

"Just stay dere til morning, and meet me at the spot at about seven o'clock."

"Why do you say dat Face, what's up?" he says.

"I gotta hit y'all off wit something and den send y'all on back down to North Carolina." I can hear someone in the background of his phone saying, "Hang the phone up baby and come fuck me."

Young says, "Here I come lil mama, hold up."

"Aye nigga are you listening to me?" I ask.

"Yeah big homie, what's up?"

"Shit man da nigga Bang, called and said he's good and to have y'all on the highway back to NC in the A.M."

"Where is he?"

"He should be about dere now, he said he was on the road when we talked a lil while ago."

"Aight it's a bet big homie, I'm gone link up with you in the morning."

"ASAP," I reply then hang the phone up.

I'm buzzing like a muthafucka, just chilling on the couch. When Shonta comes into the living room in some boy shorts, toes out, and nipples busting thru the wife beater she's wearing.

"Are you just gonna stay there all night, or are you gone come back here with me?" she says, letting the words roll off her lips seductively.

"Ma I'm fucked I ain't gone lie," I tell her, getting up slowly. But the way she's looking at me and with the alcohol in my system it's turning me on.

"Shit," I say, catching my balance.

"You're messed up baby," Shonta says placing her arm around me.

"I'm aight I got it shawty."

Giggling ... she says, "You sure?" leading the way to her room.

"I'm cool," I say, but on a real the liquor's got me feeling good.

Making it into her room I sit on the bed and lay back letting my eyes close. I heard her turning on some music then shutting her door. As I open my eyes I can see her taking off her wife beater leaving her in just a bra and boy shorts.

'Damn that shit looks good,' I think wanting a piece of her.

Climbing into the bed with me Shonta says, "Are you sleeping in yo clothes?"

"Nah but give me a min, I gotta get my thoughts together." Saying that I instantly have thoughts of Victoria pop into my mind.

"What's on yo mind that you have to get yo thoughts together?" she says, placing her hand on my chest.

"Nothing like dat, it's dis alcohol playing tricks on me."

Sliding her hand down to my wood and placing it there she says, "Take this shit off and give me this dick."

Fa real, I wanna hit the bitch but I gotta get to the crib to my girl. For some reason I just feel like laying down next to my bitch.

"You hear me?" she says.

"I hear you ma," I tell her rolling over onto my side grabbing her in my arms. "But right now let's just chill we've got all night for dat."

I know she's probably like, 'Dis nigga has got me fucked up.' But fuck it I'm bout to shake dis ho and get to my bitch.

"What you don't want dis pussy?" she says.

"Naw shawty it's not dat, but dis alcohol has got me feeling crazy like I got an upset stomach."

"Did you eat today?"

"A lil something, but not much."

"Well nigga don't throw up, in my bed."

"I'm straight just lay here wit me for a min."

Man how am I gonna shake dis bitch, I gotta get to the crib ... dozing in and out, I let out a slight snore.

Nudging me Shonta says, "Face are you asleep?"

"Naw baby," I say sitting up. "This alcohol is fucking with me dat's all."

She rolls over and faces me … "What is it I can do to make you feel better?"

Taking off my shirt, I grab her pulling her up letting her straddle me. Thru my jeans I can feel the warmth of her pussy, my penis starts to throb as I unbutton her bra.

"Unn, Face daddy," Shonta says while I'm sucking on her titties.

Gripping her breast gently as I'm sucking on her nipples like a baby. She says, "Take off your pants boo and put that dick inside me, you got me wet as fuck.

"Oh my God unn …" Saying this she gets off of me and slides her boy shorts off.

Unbuttoning my jeans I take 'em off letting 'em hit the floor. After undressing out of the rest of my clothes which basically was my boxers. I'm laying back on the bed. My buzz is still hitting me hard as hell, but I'm so focused on tearing this pussy up that I pay it no mind.

"Wait baby let me get some chocolate syrup," Shonta tells me leaving me there wit my shaft in my hand.

"Hurry up, so I can tear that muthafucka up ma," I say …

My phone rings … Ring, ring, ring, …

Looking at the screen I see Strong's number. "It's late as hell what the hell does this nigga want?" I'm thinking out loud.

"Yo what's up bruh?" I say, answering.

"Bro where the hell are you man?!" Strong says.

"On da West my nigga what's up are you aight?"

"Man I'm bout to swing thru and scoop you man, some shit went down today bruh some lil nigga came thru my shit and shook me down!"

"Hold up man slow down," I say sitting up in Shonta's bed.

"Now what the hell did you say happened …?" I say to Strong.

"A nigga came thru and put dat iron to me and robbed me for everything my nigga, do you still got dat .45 my nigga?"

"Naw man but hurry up and come thru, I'm in da Heights bruh by my mom's crib," I tell Strong.

"I'm on Tod now, so come outside, I'ma be turning into the Heights in two mins," he says.

"Aight bro," I say, getting outta Shonta's bed to get dressed.

"Yup," Strong said hanging up.

Shonta walks in with the syrup and whipped cream seeing me getting dressed, and says, "Baby what are you doing why are you putting your clothes back on?"

"Somebody robbed my nigga I gotta go!" I tell her.

With a saddened face, she says, "What do you mean you gotta go, is he okay?"

"I don't know I just know I gotta slide, he's pulling up out here any min."

Placing the syrup and cream down, she hands me my shirt and says, "Please be careful you were just in some shit the other night."

Throwing my shirt over my head, I say, "Ma I'm good just pray for the muthafuckas who fucked up.

"Damn!" I say out loud, after putting my jacket on and feeling the dope in my pocket.

"What boo?" she says looking at me.

"Here hold this til I come back ma." Handing her the work I head out of her room for the front door.

"Be safe bae!" she tells me.

"Aight," I say.

Putting my hand on the front door I notice I don't have my phone. "Shit man!" I say irritated.

"Here you forgot this," she says, once I entered her room.

Getting my phone I say, "Thanks ma come lock the door."

"Hmm baby you might need dis."

Turning around I see she has a mini-Glock P89 40 caliber handgun.

Grabbing the steel from her I'm making my way out the door.

"Boo hold up I got something else for you."

"What's dat ma?" I say.

Handing me a fully loaded extra she kisses me and says, "Baby be safe and come back."

"I got you baby girl answer yo phone when I call you."

She walks with me to the door so she can lock it, as I walk behind her I see that ass and say to myself, "I'ma tear her ass up when I get back."

CHAPTER 23

Placing the pistol on my lap after getting into Strong's car, I say, "So man what happened?"

Seeing the hammer he says, "When did you get dat bruh?"

"Strong what da fuck happened my nigga, I'm ready to go burn whoever the fuck hit you for yo shit."

"Man fa real it's crazy how dis shit happened, I really don't even know how dey knew where my shit was," Strong says.

"It's windy as fuck in dis bitch bruh roll da window up, why da hell do you got dat shit down anyway man?"

"That shit's broken, dat's what the fuck I'm saying I don't know how these niggas even knew I had my shit in here."

"What did you get hit for man?" I ask, not realizing den what really happened.

"A few ounces of that buttshit I had left of the one shit before, we went and grabbed dat shit I was testing out from yo people."

"Dat's it bro, so what did dey do after dey got da work?"

"There was some bands too, but I'm telling you somebody's been watching me or set me up my nigga."

"So who da hell you think it was Strong, cause somebody's gotta pay my nigga?"

"I don't know but I got a good feeling one of them niggas on the block's been watching me move."

"You ain't seen nobody's face or noticed nothing familiar bro?"

"Dey both had masks on but I did peep one of 'em had long hair, cause a braid was sticking out of the back of the mask," Strong says.

"Dis shit is crazy man, what time is it my nigga?"

Strong tells me, "It's about 3:40 a.m."

Thinking about my bitch, I say, "Shoot me to the crib man. We've been swerving for an hour wit dis pistol and I don't even know who we're after."

"Face who's dat new nigga that's been bleeding da block heavy wit Five lately?" Strong asks.

"Who are you thinking bout, dat young nigga Junie?"

"I think dat's him."

"Why what's up bro?"

"Shit man but, real shit I feel like dat's da muthafucka who hit me bruh."

Looking at Strong I said, "Hell naw man dat lil nigga be out dat bitch grinding my nigga."

"I'm serious dog dat nigga's been staring at me heavy when I slide thru the drive-thru, like he's on something."

"I don't know man ... Damn bro slow up you're bout to pass da house up!" I say.

Pulling into my driveway I see Vicky's car isn't here ... "Bro where's Victoria's car?" Strong asks me.

"Dat's what I was just thinking bruh, where da fuck is dis muthafucka? Oh shit, man you know what go to the Avon Oaks. She's at Kim's crib."

Still not understanding what the fuck den went down, I ask Strong, "Bruh why are you just now getting at me about dis shit?"

"Shit bro I was tied the fuck up! I thought the nigga with the braids was gonna kill me."

"So you're telling me you've been tied up, on top of them niggas robbing you bruh?"

"If it wasn't for my moms and my sister I would still be tied up now man."

"Dat's some messed up shit bro, don't trip we gon bring it to dem niggas for dis one."

Calling Vicky's phone, I tell her to open the door I'm pulling into Kimberly's parking lot.

"Aye my nigga I'ma get up wit you in a lil bit we gon get the muthafuckas who are responsible bruh," I say dapping Strong up and getting out of the car.

Noticing that his back window has been kicked out it dawns on me, that it was Five and Junie who made dat move on him. Dis shit is fucked up, cause now I'm in between a rock and a hard place wit dis one.

Scratching my head I walk into Kim's apartment to see my queen on the couch. Shutting the door I hang my jacket on the back of the kitchen chair, with the extra clip in it.

Putting the burner on safety I place it under the couch and sit down next to Vicky, she nudges me.

"Bae where have you been all day having me worrying about you?" Vicky asks me, turning on her side to give me space to lie beside her.

"Some dudes robbed Strong today, so we've been riding around looking for 'em," I tell her.

"Face you need to stay outta trouble in the middle of everybody's mess. Them niggas ain't gone ride when you're doing time and need money on your books."

Right then she made a point cause when I was just in the County, the only people who made sure I was straight was her and my grandma ...

"Vicky come on wit that shit right now aight, I already know what's up."

"Baby I'm just saying you're always being real to yo niggas what about when I need you? Where are you then?"

"Come on Victoria I hear you, but it's too late for this shit," I say, getting irritated.

"Oh you don't wanna listen to what I'm saying, huh? You're quick to jump for yo so-called homies doe!" she says, getting loud.

"Fall back man damn it's late as fuck, and Kimberly is back dere asleep. You're all loud and shit!" I shoot back at her.

"Face you must really think I'm stupid you weren't wit yo niggas all fucking day."

"I'm not on this shit I could have stayed where I was fa real you wanna be on bullshit dis late?"

"No I'm just saying don't play me like I'm dumb, I know you and I know bitches are out there on you," she says.

"Baby you're stressing bout the wrong things, we've got bigger fish to fry."

Getting up off the couch she grabs her phone and uploads to her Facebook page. I see a blunt sitting in the ash tray, and think, 'Dis girl gotta be high tryna call herself tripping out on me.'

Grabbing the blunt she lights it and sits on the other couch and asks me ...

"So who is this bitch that's all on your wall?"

"Who are you thinking about?" I say, as she leans over and pushes her phone all in my face.

"Dis bitch right here nigga."

Looking at the screen, I see it's a broad I used to chop it up wit from Sharon, PA.

The message reads: "Aww I see you're home baby boy, call my number ASAP, I hope you still remember it."

"Nigga don't just sit dere and look stupid like you don't know what's going on. So who is she Face?"

"Vicky come on dat's just a friend from Sharon, I met before I caught the County bid, fa real she's just a thought."

"So did you fuck her?"

Lying I tell her, "Nah."

"Nigga you're lying and I know you're lying, cause I've been texting her in the in box. And the ho said y'all fucked and you took her to the studio one time."

"Listen bae, I told you she's just a thought I'm not bout to go back and forth wit you tonight. Aight?"

"Just tell me did y'all have sex?"

I laid back on the sofa and said, "Good night Vicky."

Thinking of today's events I'm lying there wit my eyes closed. Dozing off I say, "Damn shit's been crazy since I got out."

"This shit is just getting started," Victoria says ashing the blunt and walking to the bathroom to make a call on her phone.

'Damn I gotta come up,' was my last thought before passing out for the night.

CHAPTER 24

"Yo what's up ma, why are you calling so late?" Jayson answered the phone.

"I wanna come see you," she says whispering into her mobile.

"What's going on, you tryna come now?" Rolling outta bed wit the beautiful stripper he left wit from the club.

"Sometime tomorrow so don't make any plans, cause I wanna be with you all day," she says to Jay, while moving a strand of hair outta her face.

Walking out onto the balcony of the hotel room Jay says, "You were just trippin' out on me earlier when we talked now you have a change of heart. What happened?"

"Nothing I just wanna be around you, I've been happy with you around. You make me happy Jay."

"So why won't you just leave dude, and come be with me?"

"It's not that easy but, you make everything feel so right," Vicky says, looking at herself in the mirror.

"Why are you whispering? Is dude around you?" Jayson asks wondering what's causing her to talk so low.

"He's in the living room asleep, and I'm in the bathroom talking to you."

"So what caused you to call me at this time of night?"

"Hold up right quick, I just heard something." Thinking it's Face knocking on the door.

"I'm using the bathroom."

"Damn bitch what are you doing shitting?"

Cracking the door, "Girl I thought you were Face's ass knocking."

"Bitch watch out I gotta use the toilet. Who are you in here talking to anyways?" Kim says, shutting the door behind her and squatting on the toilet seat.

"Dis is Jay's ass," Vic says putting her ear back to the phone.

"Hello are you still there?" she asks hoping he didn't hang up.

"Yea I'm here ma." Looking back over his shoulder at shorty who's lying butt-ass naked in the hotel bed.

"Tell Jay's ass to tell Kev I need some of the dick ASAP," Kimberly says loud enough for Jay to hear himself.

"She's been dragging my homie long enough, bout time she's tryna make something shake."

"Jay just tell him what she said without yo extra comments and shit," Vicky comments.

"Girl what did he say?" Kim says.

"'Bout time you tryna make something shake.'"

"Tell nigga I said dis my pussy and I fuck who I wanna fuck when I'm ready to fuck 'em."

"You heard dat nigga, with yo big ass ear?" Vicky says, roasting Jay about his ears being huge.

"Yeah I heard her and I'ma let him know what's up. But what else have I got dat's big besides my ears?"

"Something I'm tryna ride, if you've got time for me."

"When are you coming?"

"Hopefully tomorrow if this bitch, tryna come out there wit me tomorrow," Vicky says looking at Kim as she flushes.

"When tomorrow cause you know I've got the interview?" Kim tells Vicky.

"You'll be good, we're going after that."

"Aight cause I can use some dick in my life. I'm tired of these bitches eating my pussy."

"So what's up I'ma see you later on then shawty?" Jay's speaking breaking up their chit-chat.

"Umm yeah about 5:30 p.m. so don't get lost I'm going to call you when I hit the city," Vicky responds.

"Aight well hopefully you can get some sleep so you can be well-rested for me den baby."

"Umm unn, I'ma see you later," Vicky says ending the call.

"Bitch you are crazy talking to dat nigga while Face is out dere on the couch," Kim's saying as she opens the bathroom door.

"I know, but that nigga has got me fucked on one. Like he can mess with dese bitches out there and I'ma just lie back and wait for him to make his mind up."

Entering the living room they see Face asleep. As they make their way to the kitchen, to get a cold beverage.

"Girl I'm bout to take my ass back here to sleep." Putting her glass in the sink Kim, smacks her ass and goes to her room and back with her girlfriend.

"Bye ho," Vicky says, lying down wit Face, knowing she's got big plans for tomorrow.

Scooting over for her, "What were you doing bae, are you just now coming to lie down?" I said.

"Me and Kim were talking for a min that's all and smoked da rest of dat blunt."

"I love you boo."

"So did you fuck that bitch that's on your wall, if you love me you would tell me?"

Wrapping my arm around her, I said, "No ma I ain't do nothing with that girl."

"Whateva Face, I see it's easy for you to lie here and lie to me. In my face at dat."

"Victoria just lie here with me tonight bae and get some sleep."

"Good night Face," she tells him knowing she's going to visit Jay later on anyways.

"Good night baby."

CHAPTER 25

"Wake up bae," Vicky's shaking me saying trying to wake me up.

"Huh bae, what's up?" I say squinting my eyes looking up at her.

"Here you wanna hit this?" she says holding out a blunt for me to grab.

Sitting up and rubbing the sleep outta my eyes. I grab the blunt, before hitting it I say, "What time is it boo?"

"A lil after 11:00 a.m. There's some washed clothes and a toothbrush in the hall closet."

Passing the L back to her I get up stretch and head to the hall closet, hearing my phone ring I pick it up and continue to the back.

"Yooo what's good? I've been callin' you since seven o'clock bruh."

"What's good Young? I've been up all night man fucking wit my shawty bruh."

"Where are you my nigga? We gotta go check on dat shit dat's at the spot," Young says.

'Damn I forgot about dat,' I think to myself turning on the hot water.

"I'm over here in the Avon Oaks, I was just finna ask you where you were."

"You're deep West, my nigga whose crib are you at out dere?"

"Me and my bitch are at my girl's people's house, the water company turned our hot water off yesterday," I tell Young.

"Word bruh?" he says.

"Yeah man, come get me doe fool."

"Aight," he tells me ending our call.

Brushing my teeth I'm thinking, 'Man I hope she doesn't ask me for any money for that bill right now, I forgot bout that shit and spent the bread on that dope yesterday.'

After brushing my teeth, and washing my face. I send a text to Shonta's phone, and go back into the living room. "Shawty are you at da house I'm bout to come get dat?"

"Bae you den smoked all dat weed?" I asked Vicky.

"Kimberly got it."

Walking into the living room Kim passes me the blunt, with her friend behind her.

"What's up ugly?" I say as I take a puff on the L ...

"Shit nigga put that stupid ass gun up. You don't know who the hell is in my house or coming to my house," Kim's saying to me.

"You right Kim my bad." I grab the heat and put it in my pants, tucking it at the waistline.

Seeing Kim kiss the girl as she's exiting the door. I'm sitting there like damn is the loud playing tricks on me I know this bitch ain't just kiss the bitch.

"Yo who y'all get this loud from I'm high as a bitch?" I ask 'em.

Before, they even get the door shut 'Tat' turns around and says, "I got dat shit on deck bruh."

Hearing her speak I'm really trippin' now cause I didn't even know that was Tat this girl I grew up with.

"Yeah let me get a gram of dat shit. I ain't even know that was you fa real," I say.

"I've been saying what's up to you since I came into the living room," she says, getting the sack ready.

"My bad I ain't even pay you no attention."

"I know, but I wasn't trippin' bro."

I can see Vicky's watching me as I pull my last hundred out of my pockets, and give Tat a twenty dollar bill.

Passing me the blunt back Vicky's got a look on her face like she's ready to say something.

"You ain't got my number?" Tat says as she opens the door.

"Nah I'ma get it from Kim doe," I say passing the L to Kim.

"Aight it's on with y'all, hit me up boo," she tells Kim and closes the door.

"Damn Vicky if you're into hos, shidd let me know I'm tryna turn up wit you bae," I said looking at Vicky.

"Muthafucka don't get slapped!" Vic screams at me.

"I'm just messing wit you boo."

Kim walks to the back, into the bathroom, and Vicky comes and sits down beside me.

"Bae," she says.

"Yeah baby what's up?" I say putting the blunt in the ashtray.

"I need some money for the water bill, I called and they're telling me I still owe two hundred dollars."

Knowing I ain't got the whole two hundred dollars, I'm tryna think of a way to let her know so she doesn't complain.

"How the fuck do you owe two hundred Vicky man? Dat's crazy as fuck," I say, shaking my head.

"I don't know, but I'ma go down there and check. But I still need the money just in case Face."

My phone rings ...

"Yooo I'm coming out now bruh," I say to Young.

"Which parking lot are you in bruh?" Young asks.

"The first one my nigga."

"Come on den my nigga I'm pulling up."

Hanging up I look at Vicky ...

"Who's dat?" Vicky asks looking mad.

"One of da homies," I say.

"So you are bout to leave?"

"I gotta go do something ma."

"Well I need that money so I can do what I gotta do today."

"I'ma shoot it to you in a lil min let me catch a sale and I got you."

"A sale, with what you don't have any weed, and I know you're not pushing dope again?"

"Dat weed shit is too slow for me," I say as I put on my belongings, then adjust my belt tucking my burner.

"So you got back in the fucking game knowing the consequences that come behind that shit?"

"Bae!!!" I say.

"Face, I was just fucking out here alone for months without you for a fucking violation of your papers, and the first fucking thing you do when you get out is start moving drugs?"

"How the hell else are we gone make it out here?"

"I'm just ..."

Cutting her off. "I'm out Vicky I ain't tryna go back and forth about this with you," I said shutting the door behind me.

Stepping outside of the building, the sun is shining melting the snow a lil. I see Young and Black bobbing to music inside of the rental car, passing a spliff to one another.

Opening the back door, "X is coming for you / Can't do nothing for you /," is pumping outta the custom speakers as loud as ever.

"Bruh what's up?" Black raises his voice over the music, to speak.

"Nothing bruh turn dat down some doe," I tell him.

Passing the blunt to me Young says, "What you don't fuck with DMX my nigga?"

"Dat old ass shit bruh, hell naw dawg."

"You trippin' fool," Young protests ready to pull out of the lot.

"Hold up right fast lil bruh," I say hopping out before he could come to a complete stop.

With a light jog I got to my girl's car hoping her doors were unlocked. Opening the door I grabbed my CD's outta her whip and then I locked and closed her doors.

"Here my nigga put this in bruh," I tell Black as I get in their car and adjust myself in the seat closing the door.

"Who da hell is dis bruh?"

"Man just put da shit in and let that shit play."

Riding to the spot I'm in the back seat, just bobbing my head to the bars I be spitting.

"Bruh who is dis on here spitting like dat my nigga?" Young turned down the music and asked me.

"If I tell you I gotta kill you fam."

"Whoever the fuck it is that nigga just blanked on that track," Black says, passing the blunt back to me.

"Y'all niggas feeling that shit doe?" I ask, trying to hear their response.

"Say dat's you on dere bruh?"

"Yeah man."

"Dat shit like dat's straight up," Black tells me.

"Hands down my nigga," Young says, passing the blunt to Black.

"Y'all think that's something go to number four, 'Life is Pain' my nigga."

As we hit a few corners, til we get to the spot. Each one of us is in a zone just listening to the music play. Pulling into the driveway brings me outta my trance I was just in.

Stepping outta the car I can only imagine what was waiting in this garage for me to pick up.

Young and I go to the garage as, Black says he's got to grab something outta the house.

"Aight bro, hurry up tho cause we're in and outta this muthafucka," Young tells Black.

"Real talk, man the cops probably got a lead on this shit already," I said to Young.

Going into the garage thru the side door, I see the grill with the garbage can beside it.

"What the fuck does Bang got in this bitch, this shit stinks like dogs and shit," Young says clutching his nose.

"It's supposed to be some bread, and some work in here," I say opening the garbage pulling at the lid.

Seeing the bag I grab it, picking it up. The weight of the shit tells me there's a lot of money in it. My heart's racing with thoughts of pulling my pistol and killing Young and taking off with the money.

"I wonder how much money is in that shit," Young's saying, not even sensing the hunger and greed that's going thru my mind.

"Man I don't know, but Bang said there was some more shit here with this money."

"Y'all niggas lay it the fuck down!" Black says with a menacing look on his face ready to kill, clutching a .357 Smith and Wesson.

All I heard was "lay it the fuck down" and already knew what time it was.

"Black what's up man you gon do it like dis bruh?" Young says, fearing that it's time to say goodbye.

"Shut yo pussy ass up you like taking orders from niggas you barely know, you ain't been shit but a bitch since the day I met you," Black says drawing down on Young.

That split second was all I needed to reach for my heat in my waistline ...

Sensing the movement Black fires.

Bloud! was all he could get off before I put six hot ones in him finishing young Black for good.

Blocka! Blocka! Blocka! Blocka! Blocka! Blocka! Watching his hand release its grip from the .357, I knew he was dead.

Looking over I see Young had fallen over knocking the trash can over.

"Get up my nigga let's go!" I yell at Young.

"AGHHH nigga fuck," Young says, grabbing at his arm trying to get up.

"That muthafucka hit you bruh."

"Nah I think I just got grazed."

"Here bruh hold dis," I say, handing him the pistol, helping him up then grabbing the bag of money.

"We out man!"

"Hold up," Young says, as we step over Black's body.

Blocka! Blocka! Young puts two bullets in Black's face then spits on him.

"Ungrateful ass nigga," Young said, as we ran to the car.

"Get in the passenger seat my nigga I'ma drive," I said throwing the money into the back seat and hopping into the driver's seat.

Burning rubber all the way outta the area I didn't slow down until I was, riding past my momma's crib. Getting ready to turn onto Shonta's street.

"Damn bro this shit burns like a bitch," Young says.

Parking the rental all the way in the back of Shonta's house, we hopped out and knocked on the back door ...

CHAPTER 26

"I know this nigga sees me callin' his phone, see this shit is what pisses me off," Vicky said calling Face's phone again pressin' redial.

"Get at me after the beep," was all she heard as the voicemail picked up.

"This nigga's got me fucked up fa real Kim. Petty ass nigga knows he had that money right in his pocket when I was asking him for it."

"Girl I don't even know why you're tripping about it, we gone see Jay and Kev's ass later anyways. And bitch you know Jay's gone break bread," Kim, lets Vicky know, even though she knows it already.

"Yea cause he wants these sweet juices between my legs."

"So you know what you gotta do then."

"I shouldn't give his muthafucking ass nothing the way he was talking yesterday, when I called his ass back."

"Bitch you better not ..." Kim says.

"Girl that nigga had me hot, the way he was talking about my nigga, but what's crazy tho is it's true."

"Vicky you can't say dat cause you know Face just got out and he needs a lil time to get all the way on his feet."

"I hear you but, dat nigga's been home three or four days. He wasn't gone but four months his ass should have bread put up, what the hell was he hustling for," Vicky says, while making a turn into the gas station to fill her tank up.

"I feel what you're saying but damn bitch let the nigga get his shit together."

"Damn you're talking like you're fucking the man the way you keep speaking up for his ass," Victoria said snaking her neck at Kim.

"Ho don't try me like dat, you know I don't do niggas dat my fam fuck wit," she says, as they got out of the car.

Entering the store Vicky hands Kim sixty dollars to put in the tank. And heads to the back to get her a twenty ounce Pepsi and some Cheetos.

"Here get the gas wit this, I'm bout to get something to snack on."

"Aye grab me a Four Loco, the strawberry flavor," Kim's telling Vicky, as she gets in line.

"UGH you drink the nasty kind ho, but I got you," she says grabbing herself one as well but the lemon flavor.

Closing the cooler door she turns around and bumps into Chino. 'What the fuck?' she thinks to herself.

"Huh excuse me nigga."

"Bitch you bumped into me!" Chino says, with an attitude.

"Bitch ... You got me fucked up wit dese other bitches you talk to like dat. But nigga you ain't gone come at me sideways cause you can get it nigga. I definitely got somebody for you."

"Face bitch call dat nigga I'm on dat ho anyways, it's on site wit dat ho ass nigga."

"Muthafucka you're mad cause I ain't fucking wit you no more, now you wanna beef wit my nigga," Vicky raises her voice, causing Kim to come to her aid and assistance.

"Man Chino gon wit that shit, y'all haven't messed around in forever. What's the problem?" Kim says, getting in between the two.

"What's the problem? This bitch is popping off at the mouth, and don't even know what's going down in these streets. Her ho ass nigga shot my mans and my fucking car up the other night!"

"He should have killed your lame ass nigga!" Vicky yells over Kim's shoulder.

"Just tell him he missed and it's curtains the next time we meet," he said, flashing his forty, as he walks out of the gas station.

After paying for the snacks and Four Locos, they pump the gas and pull off.

"I don't know how I even let that muthafucka get some of this pussy," Vicky tells Kim, while driving.

Shaking her head Kim says, "I know how bitch cause you're a whore and can't handle your hormones."

"I don't know shit I had to be going thru something," Vicky said, thinking as she stopped at a red light.

"You weren't going thru anything you, just love to fill yo insides with dick."

"This asshole still hasn't called, texted or nothin' I know he's seen my missed calls," Vicky said, looking at all three cop cars heading in the same direction with sirens blaring.

"I wonder what the heck happened, girl it must be something serious cause there goes an ambulance."

"Please Lord don't let this man be the one behind all this shit today," Vicky says out loud but really to herself.

"Child go the light's been green for the longest," Kim says snatching Victoria outta her train of thoughts.

Pressing the pedal, "Kim I think something is going on, I just can't put my finger on it."

"I don't know what it is but it's hot as a muthafucka girl, somebody den got killed. Look there's another cop car heading that way," Kim says.

"Bitch that's Webber's cop car, I'd know that shit anywhere number 51. I can't stand that white pig," Vicky expressed looking in her rear view mirror.

Hearing her phone ring Kim, turns down the music ...

"Hello?"

"What's up wit you beautiful?"

"Nothing really I was just bout to grab something to eat with my girl."

"Where y'all finna eat?" Kev asks.

"I don't know, but I wish she would find somewhere so we can get off these crazy ass streets."

"Why do you say dat, what happened out there?"

"The police are everywhere, and whatever happened it's gotta be serious," Kim tells him.

"Y'all still coming down here to kick it with me and my mans today?"

"I don't know. Hold up."

Turning to Victoria, Kim asked her, "Bitch are we still going to Cleveland to fuck wit dese lames?"

'I really don't feel like it for real,' was what Vicky was gonna say until she read the text that popped up on her screen, "Bae I can't get you the two hundred right now, I'll call you later."

"Yea we're going," Victoria said.

"We'll be on our way after we get this food, and roll us one up," Kim tells Kev, while thinking about the smoke, Tat left her with earlier after eating dat kitty all night.

"Aight, it's on ma see you later."

"We'll call when we're close," she said before hanging up.

Still in her thoughts she hits the brakes just in time before, knocking the bumper clear off the car in front of her.

"Vicky are you aight girl?" Kim asked.

"I'm cool I got it my bad my thoughts were somewhere else."

"Do you need me to drive?"

"Ho I got dis I said," Vicky tells Kimberly then turns the music up before looking both ways as she makes a right turn.

Pulling into Perkins off of Elm Road Victoria finds a place to park.

"Kim you know this bitch, texted me talking about he can't give me the hundred."

"Why the hell he ain't just call you?"

"You're asking me like I can answer that, hell I don't know why he didn't call."

Shutting the door to the car, "Well who knows but let's enjoy this food before we hit the road," Kim said, while putting her purse on her shoulder.

"Aye Kim go ahead and find us a spot to sit, I'm bout to use the restroom."

"I got you," she responded knowing her cousin was only going in there to call Face.

'Why isn't he picking up the damn phone?' Vicky thought as she redialed his number.

Ring, ring, ...

"Get at me after the beep," the answering service picked up.

"Nigga when you come looking for me, I hope you can find me," was the message left on his voicemail before Victoria hung up and walked out to find Kimberly.

Right as she sat down, the waitress came to their table.

"Are you ladies ready to order yet?"

"Ummm can you give us a minute please?"

"No problem I'll be right over there when you're ready."

"Thanks, I appreciate you," Victoria said.

CHAPTER 27

"Oh my God what happened?" she says, as she steps back from the door letting us in.

"Come on my nigga," I say to Young, leading him to the bathroom.

"AHHHHHH Damn my shit is on fire it feels like I can't even move my shit bruh," Young tells me clutching his arm tryna relieve the pain he's feeling.

Getting to the bathroom, I turn on the water to the sink and tell my homie to sit down.

"Fuck dawg you're losing a lot of blood my nigga," I said as I run the washcloth under the water.

"I know man I thought the bullet just grazed me," Young says sitting on the toilet seat.

"Take off yo shirt let me check the wound, and let's hope you were just grazed."

Slipping his good arm out of its sleeve, then tryna get his good arm thru Young hardens his face and says, "I can't do it bruh, my shit is messed up."

Looking into his eyes I can tell my man's fucked up pretty badly.

"I got you homie just sit back."

As I'm helping him outta his shirt, Shonta's standing at the door. "Do y'all want me to help?" Shonta asks, grabbing the rag and applying pressure to the wound as I drop his shirt to the floor.

"Look Shonta do you know what you're doing?" I asked.

"I swear I hope she does bruh, this hurts man," Young speaks up.

"Is he going to have to go to a hospital?"

Wiping at the blood and looking at the wound before applying pressure again, she says, "Naw I don't think he will have to, it looks like it just went in and out thru the top of the shoulder."

"I knew you were hit my nigga, that was too much blood for you to just be grazed homie."

"I don't give a fuck just help me baby girl, do whatever you need to do to stop the bleeding and patch me up just do it," Young said, as he leaned his head back.

"You'll be aight I'ma do what I can for you. Face reach in the cabinet right there and get the peroxide, and a new bar of that soap in there."

Retrieving what she just told me to get for her, I turn around and set it down on the sink countertop. "What else are you gonna need?" I asked, knowing that she's gonna need a first aid kit.

"Go in my room and there's a first aid kit in my dresser, grab that and the Ace bandage patch and bring them to me," Shonta tells me looking sexy as fuck as she gets my lil nigga right.

"Do you have any pain meds I can take? This shit is burning like a bitch ma."

Yelling to the back, she says, "Face look in my purse and grab those percs outta the inside pocket!"

Seeing the purse I look thru it and find the pills I grab five of 'em and leave the other seven, and head back to the bathroom.

"Here you go baby girl." I put the kit and Ace bandage on the sink and watch her go to work.

"Bruh you grab the percs?" Young looks up at me.

"My fault my nigga there's five of 'em right here bruh."

Without water to chase 'em down Young pops all of the muthafuckas back.

"You ain't got no smoke bruh, roll up? Dat bitch ass nigga Black had mine in his pocket when we murked dat fuck nigga."

"Yea I got some, but let me get that bag out on the back seat first."

"Aye shawty that shit bites when you touch it right ..." I could hear my homie say as I walked out of the bathroom to the back door to go grab the money in the bag.

As I put the bag of money on the living room table, I take the weed outta my pocket.

"Shonta you got some shells in here so I can roll up?" I ask, as I wonder where all her kids are.

"Here's one in my pocket," Young says and passes it to me.

"Y'all almost done?" I ask shorty.

"I'll be finished in five minutes," she responds.

By the time I finished rolling the blunt, and dumping the guts of the cigarillo in the trash my mans was walking out with his arm wrapped up and shirtless.

"You ain't lit that shit yet my nigga?" Young says as he sits down next to me.

"Here bro light it right quick."

"You got a lighter?"

Passing him the lighter, I open the bag to see what's inside. My heart's racing as I'm lost in thought looking at all the money in the bag.

"Man bruh look at this shit," I tell Young as I dump all the stacks of paper outta the garbage bag and onto Shonta's living room table.

"Face that's gotta be over one hundred grand my nigga, fa real I ain't think Bang was eating like dat you feel me?" Young tells me.

Shonta walks in from washing herself off and cleaning the bathroom up from all of the blood. "Holy shit where did y'all get all this money from?" she says stopping in her tracks stuck on all the stacks laying on the table in front of her.

"It's best you act like you don't even see all this shit ma, that way you don't know shit if those people come knocking on yo door."

Coughing ...

"Here bruh take this blunt, that shit is some fire. Where did you get that from?" Young passes me the L.

"Some bitch, dat's a dike ho."

"You got her number we need some more of dis?"

"I think so," At the mention of her number I realized I didn't have my phone on me.

Running to the car I opened the door and my phone was sitting between the driver's door and the driver's seat just beeping alerting me that I have voicemails to check.

Going back into the house, I hit the blunt one more time and passed it to Shonta.

"What are you finna do wit all this money?" Shonta asked.

"Count it," I said.

Before the blunt was even finished, the pills kicked in and put my lil homie out for the count.

"Shonta where's the ashtray?"

"Huh?" she says, putting all the money that's been counted back in the bag.

"Where's yo ashtray, so I can put this shit out?"

"Oh, here you go. I didn't hear you that shit got me high."

Grabbing the tray outta her hand, I say, "Or is it all this money?"

My phone beeps again, I look at the screen and it's a text message from Vicky.

"You don't wanna answer yo phone bitch?"

I don't even text back I just put the phone back on the table and get back to counting.

An hour later the total comes out to one hundred and eighty-three stacks.

"Where are yo kids?" I say to Shonta as I grab the bag and head to her room.

"My mother has them they'll be back in bout forty minutes, she said they were coming back at three p.m."

"What time is it now?" I can see her behind me as I turn to go in her room as I looked in the mirror on her dresser.

"Two-nineteen p.m."

"Look don't let nobody come in here when I leave, I'ma need to put the bread up for a lil minute until I make my move later on."

"You don't have nothing to worry about boo I got you."

Turning around from her closet after putting the paper up, I see Shonta bent over getting one of her children's shoes off the floor. A thought flashed thru my mind of how I was about to bust her open last night before I got that call from my man Strong.

My shaft having a mind of its own I instantly get hard and walk up behind her as she's standing back up and turning around to face me.

"You wanna finish what we started last night?" I say, kissing her soft lips not giving her a chance to respond, as my hands explore her body.

Gripping her ass cheeks, while walking her backwards to her queen-sized bed. She lets out a soft moan in my ear while I kiss and suck on her neck.

"UHHH, take dis pussy daddy," Shonta tells me while thoughts are racing through her mind of all the money I just counted in front of her.

Caressing her body and grinding on her, she's had enough and pushes me off her and pulls her shirt off.

"Daddy come get this pussy, I wanna feel you inside me."

Taking off my jeans, my penis is stiff as fuck and I can feel the pre-cum seeping out of the head of my dick.

"Damn baby I'm bout to tear this pussy up," I said as I eased her outta her booty shorts.

She had no panties on, so that only made shit a lot easier for me.

Coming outta my briefs, I climbed on top of her teasing her as I slid my dick up and down on her clit.

"You ready ma?"

"OHHH shit, Face hold up bae let me suck it first boo."

An hour later I'm smacking her on her ass as she gets up to take a shower.

"Aye lil bruh? Get up my nigga we gotta figure out what we gone do with the bread bruh," I holla at Young stirring him outta his peaceful sleep.

"Huh bruh," Young sits up saying rubbing sleep out of his eyes.

"Man this nigga Bang just texted my line, saying, 'What's good.' I hit him back saying, 'Shit all bad.'"

"Fuck my nigga them percs put me down bruh, but fa real I wouldn't be surprised if he don't call you right now," Young says.

"How is your shit feeling lil bruh?"

"I'm in pain like a muthafucka. Aye but how much is that bread coming out to fooly?"

"One hundred and eighty-three stacks."

"Call that nigga Bang, and let him know the scoop. And tell him I said I'll be on my way tomorrow."

"It's a bet, here put this jacket on my nigga," I said tossing him my jacket.

"Who is that at the door?" Young said slipping the jacket on.

Peeking out of the curtains on the living room window I see we have children getting out of the car. Hearing shawty getting out of the shower, and going to her room I walk back to her room and tell her that her kids are home.

Putting on some sweats with a T-shirt she, goes to the living room just as they are coming thru the front door. Her moms must have had keys to the house.

"Who is this?" the oldest child says, to her mother.

"Why are you being nosy, what did I tell you about that?"

"I was just asking mom, dang," the oldest one said.

"Who are you danging, and take that jacket off," Shonta ordered.

"I'm hungry!" Booty, her second oldest yells.

"Stop all that muthafucking screaming. And bring your ass in this kitchen."

Walking out from the back I speak to Shonta's mother, and her oldest Zay.

"What's up Face?" Shonta's mother Venes says.

"Aye bro, come back here right quick," I tell Young.

"Shut the door bruh."

"What's good?" Young turns around and said after shutting the door.

"I just talked to Bang, he's talking bout just shooting him one hundred and forty racks up dere, right but look I'ma give you fifteen thousand bruh. Dat's cool?" making eye contact as I asked.

"Real talk bruh I ain't trippin' I know you just got home and need to get your hand right," Young's telling me.

"Do y'all got some more smoke?" Shonta walks in asking.

"Yea boo roll dis lil shit up," I respond as I fish the lil bit of loud outta my pocket.

"Boo? So I'm yo boo now?" she puts her hand on her hip.

"Do you wanna be?" passing the loud to her as I asked.

"Boy you are crazy. Don't you have a bitch?" she says looking back as she walks out of the room to go roll up.

"Aye my nigga I'm not bout to slide down dere to fuck with Bang til tomorrow or later on tonight."

"Hit that nigga up and tell him, cause da nigga talked like he wanted you to come ASAP," I tell him as I took the money out of the closet to slip out what we had coming to us.

"I'ma see what's up wit him in a minute," Young exclaims, as he took off his jacket studying his shoulder.

"Aye quit fucking wit that shit bruh," turning around seeing Young fucking wit his wound.

Ring ... Ring ... Ring ... Looking at my screen I see Vicky's number.

"Damn man dis bitch has been blowing me up." I pressed the end button saying, really out loud but Young heard me.

"Who was dat bruh?" Young looks at me quizzing.

"My wifey, but you know how dat shit goes, one minute we're on good terms the next we're beefing."

"I can feel it big bruh."

"What are you bout to do with dis money?" I ask as I handed him the fifteen grand.

"It ain't no telling, but you wanna know something?" Young says, looking at me.

"What's up bruh?" I said, as I take my twenty-eight grand out of the bag.

"I ain't gone fuck it up, cause dis da first few thousand I had to stretch a muthafucka over bruh."

"Me too," shaking my head, closing the bag up.

"Better him den us, even doe that was da homie."

"Dat's what greed gets you lil homie."

Young stands up and said, "All money ain't good money."

Ring ... Ring ... Ring ...

Pushing the end button again I said, "I know my nigga."

CHAPTER 28

"Are you ready girl?" Kim says, to Vicky who's been calling Face for the past five mins.

"Yea come on but, this nigga's got me fucked up Kim," she says, getting up walking to the cash register to pay for their meals.

"Thank you come again," the cashier tells them as they leave.

"We're bout to kick it tonight, we're not coming back til tomorrow," Victoria plots as she opens the door to the driver's side.

"I'm down bitch you already know, and I might give Kev's ass some of this good-good tonight. Depending on how I'm feeling after we go out if he hasn't gotten on my nerves by then."

"Cut it out ho, you know you wanna know what da muthafucka's pipe game is like."

"As long as it ain't like that wack-ass game he be tryna spit he'll be aight. But he is cute tho."

Vicky gives Kim an eye, then busts out into a laugh.

"Bitch what's so funny?" Kim's asking knowing already why she's laughing.

"I know you ain't say he was cute."

"Ho stop cause that muthafucka you're choppin' it with ain't no better."

"Why ain't he?" Vicky says looking to her right at Kimberly.

"Girl slow yo ass down before you miss the turn."

Slowing down and making their turn emerging onto the ramp, that takes them onto the highway Victoria says, "... And why ain't he?"

Kimberly shoots her a look that says, 'Girl please.'

They both bust out laughing ... Catching her breath Vicky said, "You're a mess bitch, but fuck it they got that money and I need mines."

"Me too shit if Kev's ass is thinking that he's getting some, he's coming off something."

Hearing the ring tone she has set for Jay she picks up her phone only hoping that it was her man, but fuck it Jay will do for now ...

"Hello bae, what's up?" Victoria answers.

"Oh yeah, it's bae now all of a sudden?" Jay exclaims.

"What you don't like it when I say that, cause I ain't gotta say it?"

"It's not that I'm just wondering what's gotten into you now, just a minute ago it wasn't bae."

"Nothing has gotten into me, I'm just happy I'm coming to see you. I'm excited that I'm bout to be in your presence."

"When are you gonna be here baby?" Jay asks, wanting to be ready for Vicky when she gets there.

"Nigga you were just talking bout me calling you bae, now you're calling me baby."

"You've always been my baby, you're the one who switched up on me ever since your man got out or whatever."

Shaking her head, "Jay let's not talk about that, please you know how I feel about that but there's obviously a connection between you and I if I'm on the highway coming to see you right?"

"I feel you ma, but look just hit me when you hit my city baby girl."

"Yo city, nigga don't forget I was born and raised in da land," Vicky protested.

"I respect it ma, so how long do you think you're gone be before you touch down?" Jay asked, so he would know how long he had to wash off the juices of the ho he just fucked and be ready for a night out in the city with his boo.

"Give me bout forty-five mins to an hour, you know this weather is bad."

"Aight boo, hit me when you touch down." Ending their call and, walking out from the back room of the broad's crib that he was at.

"Okay," she says and hits the end button, tryna play in front of Kim. But she knows Jay really hung up on her.

Hitting her left blinker, she looks at Kim after switching lanes.

"So where do you think we should go out to tonight ho?"

"Somewhere down in the flats," Kim says, thinking.

"What do you think about Club Sin?"

"I'm down wit it, I heard that shit is where it's at fa real doe."

"So we'll hit Sin, then top it off with Chrissy's. That's cool wit you?" Victoria says, but asking her cusin at the same time.

"The strip club bitch you're a freak fa real ain't you?"

"And you know this, shidd bitch I miss those days when I worked in a club," she speaks while thinking bout those long nights at the strip club.

"I bet Face used to wanna kick your ass too, I know he hated that shit."

"Hell yeah he hated that shit. We even stopped fucking around for a while for dat shit. But I wasn't bout to stop making my money to chase his ass."

"Y'all done came a long way tho Vicky, I remember when you first started fucking wit his ass."

"I know bitch he used to have me wrapped around his finger, bad as hell," Vicky thinks back.

"Yes you had dat shit bad too, y'all wouldn't be together months but soon's he called you would drop everything and go running."

"Shut up, was it dat bad fa real?"

"Yes bitch and you know it."

"I don't give a damn, and I would still do it now," Vicky tells, Kim while turning up the music so they could enjoy the rest of their drive.

"You ain't gotta go home tonight / You can stay right here wit me /," they sang along to Monica and DMX's song 'Don't Gotta Go Home.'

"This is my shit cuz start this shit over," Kim yells over the beat.

"And this is exactly how I'm feeling right now," Vicky said as they replayed the song over.

"Stop thinking bout that boy and let's enjoy ourselves out here tonight."

"You're right but, damn his ass could have at least returned my calls, you know like I know he saw that I've been calling him all day."

Ignoring Vicky, Kimberly says, "Call and see which exit we need to be getting off on, shit ain't nobody thinking bout you and Face's bullshit."

"Ho I know which exit to take, how many times have we been down here?" She looks at the signs on the side of the road to see if her exit is near.

"So you just know they're gone be at his house?"

"I don't know, but what does that sign say 2 miles til Exit 4B 95th and Huff?"

"Yup," Kim said, taking out her phone to text Kev to see where he is.

Shifting lanes so she could depart on the approaching exit Vicky turns the music down. "Kim call and see where they are."

"Kev just texted and said come to his house," Kim says lying back in her seat.

"And where does his ass stay bitch?" she asks stopping at the light at the end of the ramp.

"On 93rd and Miles, in E.C."

"Aight, call Tiara and see if she wants to meet us and have a drink once we get to the bar."

"I'ma text her, cause I don't feel like talking fa real. I think I got a headache."

"There's some Tylenols in my purse," Vicky said before making a left in pursuit of their destination.

CHAPTER 29

"What happened to him?" Strong said, as I got in the front seat and Young slid into the back, of his whip.

"He got shot earlier he's good doe the shit just went in and out. Young dis Strong, Strong dis my lil homie Young." I introduced the two and Strong pulled out into traffic.

"Aye do you know where I can get pain meds percs, vikes, or tabs?" Young says, reaching for the Black and Mild.

"I've got some percs at my crib bruh, we're bout to pull up over dere in a second after we catch dis bop. You brought that work wit you bruh?" Strong asked Face, as he pulled into a driveway unknown to Face and Young.

"What do you need bruh?" I said, reaching for the dope in my pocket.

"I think this nigga wanted a quarter."

"You ain't got a scale in here, so I can weigh dis shit bruh?"

"Aye homie, grab dat digital right dere in the pocket of my seat bruh," Strong says to Young looking at him in the rearview mirror.

Passing forward the scale Young said, "Bruh turn the heat up a lil bit."

"I got you homie. I'ma hit dis nigga two fifty for the cutie you ain't gotta shoot me nothing my nigga get on yo feet," Strong says not knowing anything bout his and Young's inheritance.

After weighing up the seven grams I give Strong the work and he goes into the unknown house to bust the sale.

"Aye bruh you gone be cool on the road tomorrow?"

"I'ma be good I'ma need some pills tho for the drive, but other than that the rest ain't nothing I play that freeway bruh," Young's saying to me, while passing the Black and Mild.

"Dat rental is hot as fuck you gotta leave that shit parked til you're ready to slide in the morning."

"Shawty ain't trippin' bout you letting me leave it over dere, is she?"

"Ma's a trooper my nigga she's down for whatever, but she can't do a bid with a nigga. You'd be good for a few months but as soon as you're in bid mode baby girl den moved around to the new nigga dat's getting money."

"So why did you leave all dat cash over dere?" Young says.

"I neva said she was stupid I said she's a trooper, do I have to say more?"

"I feel you bruh," he says, then reaches for his shoulder squinting from the pain shooting thru him.

Opening the driver's door Strong hops back in handing me my paper, I shoot him fifty for making me the sale.

"Good looking bro," Strong's saying as my phone rings.

"Hello?" I answered.

"What's good Face, are you good bruh?" the caller said.

"Who is dis?" I asked, before recognizing the voice.

"Dis is Pimp bruh, are you aight out dere? I heard shit's real bruh muthafuckas are capping like dey really bout that action."

"I got shit in order, bruh you know how I get down fam. Dis shit is only built for a thorough breed my nigga," I told my cusin P.I., informing him that there ain't no need for him to shoot down to the city.

"Aight man stay in touch I'm only two hours away, if anything jumps off I'ma be dere ASAP," he tells me.

"Already bruh," I reply.

"One love."

"One love."

"Y.T. my nigga!" he said before hanging up.

Pulling into Strong's driveway, I see his Chrysler with the window busted out in the back.

"Let's step in here for a minute, and smoke. I got a few bops bout to come thru," Strong said turning off the car and stepping out.

About an hour and a half den passed, we're on our fourth cigarillo filled with kush. When I noticed that Strong den ran thru two ounces of heroin.

"Dat boy is moving like dat my nigga, you just moved a zip and a half, and we haven't even been over here two hours."

"Face dis is where da money is I tried to tell you, shit I just ran thru two ounces and somebody else just called for a few more grams," Strong said.

"Dem niggas who robbed you ain't get everything, they couldn't have the way you're making this shit look," I said, looking at Young who held the blunt to his lips.

"You know I had something in the stash to bounce back off of."

"Dang y'all niggas ain't hungry?" Young said passing the blunt to Strong.

"There's a pizza spot down the street, we can shoot up dere after dis play comes thru bruh," Strong said, puffing away at the weed.

"You're talking bout Carman's?" I asked.

"I definitely ain't talking bout Little Caesar's, that shit is trash."

"I'm starving dawg!" Young says.

"Nigga you need to be tryna get some rest, you gone be on da road all day tomorrow," I tell him, then hit the kush.

"How the hell did you get shot my nigga?" Strong said before getting up to answer the knock on the door.

"What's up wit bruh asking all dese questions and shit?"

"He's good people my nigga don't trip," I tell Young, passing him the blunt of kush.

"Aight shidd, y'all ready to shoot up here to Carman's?" Strong says, after coming back to the living room from making his sale.

"Hell yeah my nigga."

"Let's go den, before another one of these muthafuckas gets to calling."

So while we waited for the pizza to get made, Young and I filled Strong in about what went down.

"Dat's fucked up, I bet y'all ain't even think nothin' like dat was bout to go down."

"Man fuck no, and fa real there was pose to be some work with the money, but how dat shit happened we ain't have time to get the shit," I said.

Getting up to go see if the orders were ready, I peeped this bad redhead I used to try to rap with before I got jammed up.

"Here's your orders, do you need drinks with them?" redhead asked, while looking at me with her pretty smile batting her sexy eyes.

"Ummm yeah three cherry sodas please."

While she filled the drinks up, and rang up the orders, I was stuck in thought trying to remember baby girl's name.

"It'll be fifteen dollars and seventy-nine cents," redhead spoke breaking my train of thought.

Reaching into my pocket I pulled out a hundred dollar bill that I got from the bop Strong made for me.

"Here you go lil mama," I said.

"Your change is eighty-four dollars and twenty-one cents, thanks for coming to Carmen's."

"You're welcome, but am I tripping or do you look real familiar?"

"Don't act like your lil bid in the County made you forget who I am."

"I apologize but I just gotta ask, what's your name again beautiful?"

"OMG really, I know you didn't just ask that fa real Face."

'Wow this bitch knows who I am fa real,' I thought.

"What's wrong a cat got your tongue?" redhead says.

"Naw it ain't that I'm just tryna place the right name with the right face," I said, seeing my homies looking in on my conversation with shorty.

"Christina, don't let the pizzas burn from being in the oven too long," I heard her supervisor say.

"I'm getting them out now," she yells back.

"AHHH Christina I thought that's what it was," I said as she turns to the oven giving me a show worth watching.

"Boy you wouldn't have known if you hadn't heard my supervisor just say it."

"How would you know I ain't even get a chance to tell you ma, best trust me I wouldn't forget a smile as sexy as yours."

"You're full of it," she says.

"I know, but look I'ma let you get back to work hopefully I can see you around soon doe ma."

"Hopefully," Christina says, then walks off twitching the hell out of her ass like she just knew I was watching.

"Damn homie are you aight?" Young said, walking up grabbing his personal box of pizza with his drink.

"I'm good my nigga, I just really forgot who baby girl was for a min. But aye tho this one's yours right here my nigga," letting him know he grabbed the wrong shit.

"Man I'm as hungry as a bitch," he says, getting his food.

"After seeing all that ass on her I couldn't give a fuck bout the pizza, I want some of that juicy ass on her."

"You would eat that bitch's pussy right now Face?" Strong asks, getting his box outta my hand as we head for the car.

"Fuck it bruh, I'ma eat the fuck outta dat ho right now my nigga."

"You're a nasty muthafucka man, but I can't cap doe bruh I might have too."

"Strong you just ain't made no sense, how am I a nasty muthafucka but you just said you might eat da bitch out too?"

"Bruh do got a point doe Strong," Young jumps in on the conversation.

"Hell yeah dat's money bum!" I said popping the back of the collar of Strong's shirt, and snatching at the back of his neck in a quick motion.

"See money get money," Young says, and does the same.

"I don't play that money shit bro, muthafuckas putting their hands on my neck and shit," Strong says.

"Go to trial den bum."

Laughing at Strong as we walk out the door of Carmen's to the car, I asked, "What time is it my nigga?"

"Ten til," Strong lets me know.

"What nine o'clock?" Young asks.

"Yup."

"Bruh what time are you gone be tryna hit the road?" I asked Young.

"I don't know, probably in the AM, like five in the morning."

"Aye go back West to Shonta's crib," I tell Strong as we slide into his car.

"Check the glove compartment and see if that .38 snub nose is in there," Strong says, looking at the car that pulled into the lot.

Giving him the three eighty I peep what his attention is focused on.

"Who the fuck man?" I asked as he takes the gun.

"It looks like the muthafuckas that robbed me," he says gripping the pistol.

Taking my strap from my waistline I prayed, 'Please don't let this be who I think it is.'

"Young look when I hop out and run up on them muthafuckas you hop in the front seat and get ready to pull off," Strong says, starting the car.

"I got you bruh, just make sure you done leave no witnesses," Young said.

Seeing movement behind the tinted windows of the box Chevy, the niggas that Strong thinks are his enemies I asked, "Bruh how do you know that it's them?"

Not responding he hops out of the driver's side door, with me right behind him coming around the car to get in position for a clear kill shot. Young jumps in the driver's seat and has the gears switched with his foot on the brake ready to go.

The dudes in the Chevy don't see us coming looks like they're looking down at something, I still see movement tho as my palms begin to sweat from the adrenaline rush of this shit all happening so fast.

This shit all happened in one quick motion, Strong swings the door of the passenger side open as I reach the driver's door.

Sounds of women screaming their hearts out could be heard miles away.

"AHHHHHHH!!!!! Please don't shoot us!" the driver said.

"OHH my God!" another exclaimed outta fear from the back seat, wiping her nose of the powdery substance.

Snatching at the driver's door it doesn't open up. "Open the fucking door bitch, before I shoot this bitch up!"

"It's broken, I had to get in thru the other side!" the driver yells.

"What the fuck are y'all in here doing tooting powder up y'all damn noses?" Strong said to the girls.

"Please don't hurt us man, I got kids out here that need me," the passenger protested.

Reaching for the back door pulling it open, I see cocaine all over the chick's fucking clothes and back seat.

"Nobody's gonna do nothing to y'all, aight? Look just act like nothing happened tonight and you ladies will get home to your kids and quit doing drugs."

"Okay I promise this will never get out, just let us make it," the driver said, looking back at me with her hands up.

"What's your name ma?" I asked the driver.

"Shirley," she says with a look of horror in her eyes.

"Whose car is this Shirley?" Strong asked her.

Looking at Strong, she sees he wants blood, so she hesitates.

"Bitch whose fucking car is this, don't make me say it again!"

Shirley starts, crying and breathing heavily panicking and shit.

"It's her boyfriend's! Please don't shoot her," the passenger said.

"What's his name?" Strong clenches his teeth, I'm starting to believe he's bout to shoot one of these hos.

"Jun ... Jun ... Junie!" Shirley said, covering her face with her hands bursting into tears.

"You tell Junie I got a message for him," Strong said with a menacing look on his face.

"Y'all let's roll!" Young yells, out the door of Strong's whip.

Cocking back his gun Strong aims his gun, all the girls' eyes are big as saucers at this point, and I could have sworn none of 'em are even breathing.

"Bruh let's go," I said before this dumb nigga shoots one of these bitches.

Boom! The gun goes off.

Shattering, the glass of the front windshield breaks flying everywhere.

"Nooooo please don't do this please," the passenger says looking Strong in his eyes.

"Bruh let's roll, now!" I yelled, bringing my boy back outta his zone.

You could hear them hos crying and shit as we ran back to the car. I can bet you that's a high they'll never forget.

"Man what the hell is wrong wit you my nigga? You aight bruh?" Young questions Strong.

"I'm straight homie just whip this muthafucka to my crib and park in the garage, we gotta switch cars!"

Sitting in the back seat I can see Strong's chest moving up and down, from the heavy breathing caused by his adrenaline rush. I just thank God that my young niggas weren't in that car just now.

CHAPTER 30

"We're pulling up in front of your house now. Are y'all ready or do you want us to come inside?" Kim's asking Kev.

"Okay well come on don't have us waiting all night out here we tryna enjoy our night," she said hanging up on Kev.

"Pull in right here behind Jay's whip."

"What did he say they were doing?" Vicky says, parking behind the car in front of her.

"Nothing about to lock up the crib and come outside so we can roll out."

"So did Tiara hit you back yet and let you know if she's coming out to sip with us or nah?"

"This is her ass calling right now ... Hello?" Kim answered.

"What's up bitch bring yo ass on and meet up with us ho," Vicky yells, in the background.

"She said shut yo loud ass up Vicky," Kim says.

"Tell that ho I said bring her stinky ass girlfriend with her too," Vicky responded.

"Girl aight bye," Kim tells her sister hanging up the phone.

"What did that heffer say?" Vicky asks.

"Nothin' she heard you," Kim said back.

Hearing a knock on the back door of the car, startled them lil.

"Who the hell is that?" Vicky says looking back tryna see in the dark.

"Kevin's nothing ass unlocked the door."

"Boy who are you walking up on like dat out here, you don't know you'll get dealt with out here don't forget I'm from Cleveland nigga?" Vicky said as Kev slid into the back seat.

"My bad I didn't mean to scare y'all," Kev comments.

"Scare nigga please you better recognize what she just said," Kim shoots back at him.

"Okay den my fault I was just sayin' doe."

"You're good, but where is Jayson's sexy self?" Vicky said seeing headlights pull in behind her car and park.

Looking back Kev says, "That's him right dere I think." He was hoping she didn't know Jay had just went and dropped a female off.

"I hope so cause I'm not tryna be waiting on his ass all night," Kim comments.

"Fa real a bitch is tryna kick it tonight, I'm not finna be up here just sitting around," Victoria added.

Ring ... Ring ... Vicky looks at her phone seeing it's Jay's number and answers.

"Hello, where the hell are you boo?"

"Is that your car in front of me ma?" Jay says, sitting behind the steering wheel turning the ignition off after spraying himself with Polo cologne tryna hide the other woman's fragrance from Vicky.

"Yea, what are you doing? I'm ready to go out and have some fun."

"Here I come ma let me lock my doors, unless y'all want me to drive?"

"We aight, just come on my cousin is bout to come up so we can have a few drinks."

"Aight baby girl here I come now," Jay said hanging up.

"Bitch get in the back my boo is bout to ride up front," Victoria tells Kim.

"You shitty ho, don't start acting funny," Kim replied stepping out to get in the back with Kev.

Getting in the passenger seat Jay greets everybody.

"What's up wit y'all? Y'all ready to step out right now?"

"Uh huh, I'm tryna get in my zone and out of dis damn car," Kim said.

"How do we get to Club Sin from here bae?" Vicky asked.

"Bae, you must have a motive behind dat?" Jay replied.

"Don't try me like dat," she tells him.

"How am I trying you I'm just saying ma?"

"You know what you're doing, well tryna insinuate."

"Why are you starting with me already ma, we ain't even got our night started yet?" Jay leans over and kisses Victoria on the cheek.

"Which way do I go to get to the bar?"

"Here just let me drive ma I got you," Jay tells her, opening his door to change her positions.

"Yo muthafucking ass better not wreck my shit nigga," Victoria said getting out.

"Bruh, do you still have some loud on you?" Kev asks, cuddling next to Kimberly.

Putting the car in gear, "I got a lil something my nigga. Why what's good?" Jayson stated.

"Naw, I was just seeing, I've got a lil something too doe."

"We should be straight bruh."

"It's a bet," Kev says then whispers in Kim's ear as he palms her ass.

"What's up wit you tho, ma are you staying with me tonight?" Jay says to Vicky while stopping at the stop sign looking both ways.

Thinking for a min about Face, she says, "I don't know I'll let you know before the night's over."

"I'll accept dat." Hoping he can win her over by the end of tonight.

"Roll up Kev, so we can blow one before we step into the club," Vicky looks back at Kev and Kim with their lips locked in between each other's.

"I knew he was gon get yo ass bitch, get her ass Kev. Dat ho gone give that pussy up tonight huh bro?" Vicky says, laughing at the two engaged with each other.

Stopping for a second to shut Vicky up, Kimberly says, "Dis nigga is gone work for dis pussy, trust me bitch."

"Dat's all it's gone take, well consider it done ma," Kevin tells his baby girl, then reaches up front to pass Vicky the bud to roll up.

"Ma you still have my mix tape in here?" Jayson said referring to his CD.

"It should be I'll find it," Vicky answered.

"Don't let me find out ya nigga don thru my shit out da window."

"So you're on joke time right now talking shit, huh?"

"I'm just saying it's been in here for weeks all of a sudden it's gone now that yo people's done got out."

"That damn CD is in here somewhere, don't come in here starting no shit about a damn CD. I just wanna enjoy my night with you Jay and you get in here stressing a muthafucka about a fucking mix tape already," she snaps looking in the console to see if his CD's in there. Instead she takes out an envelope from some mail she got the other day and continues to break the weed Kev gave her on it.

What the hell happened to this man's CD? "Jay look in the side of that door boo and see if it's there."

Reaching his hand down to search for the mix tape as he drives, he feels it. Pulling the disc up and looking at it. "Damn shawty is dis how you do my joint, where is the case?"

"It's in here somewhere, you're just gone keep finding something to talk shit about. Put da shit in the player nigga and relax dang," Vicky said, now twisting up the loud pack.

"OMG! Y'all two just chill and let's get to this club so we can turn up," Kim says, while sliding her hand into Kev's pants feeling his rock hard penis.

Hearing their music come thru the speakers of the LeSabre Kevin said, "Bruh put that shit on six and turn it up."

"I got you my nigga," Jay told him, while changing lanes so they could get to their destination.

In the mean time while they smoked, Vicky's phone alerts her showing she has a text coming in from her man. Grabbing her phone looking at the message she sees Jay looking in her direction at her reading her message.

But not even replying back she, puts her phone away and says, "Duh watch the road before you wreck why are you all up in mines?"

"You know what, you're right shawty," Jay replied after taking a toke of the blunt and passing it to them in the back.

CHAPTER 31

"Be safe out here my nigga, and call me if you need me homie," I said getting out of Strong's car just after sending the text out to Vicky.

"Fa sho' bruh I'ma get at you. Young drive carefully when you hit dat highway lil homie," Strong told us.

Closing the door and stepping off to the side Young said, "Homie I can fuck wit that nigga dere he's bout his paper and he's bout dat life."

"Dat's a good man right dere Young da nigga will give you his last, a spot to lay yo head at all dat my nigga. But for some reason I feel like my homies Five and Junie, da muthafuckas who robbed him doe."

"How would you figure dat Face?" Young's curiosity led him to ask.

Knocking on the back door to Shonta's house, I looked at my lil homie.

"Trust me I know bruh, and dat's fucked up. But you know there ain't no loyalty dese days niggas let greed get the best of 'em."

Shaking his head, Young sees his car still parked where he left it and thought of Black.

"Why didn't you call before you came back baby?" Shonta asked after opening the door seeing who it was.

"I told you I'll be back when I left earlier."

"Okay but how did you know I was gonna be home Face?"

"You're home ain't you?" I responded back walking into the house with Young in tow.

"I guess, Young how is your shoulder feeling?" Shonta iggs Face, and checks on Young.

"I'm good fa real, the shit is biting a lil bit but nothing to sweat about."

"Yo Shonta who all is over here wit you?" Looking at her sexy ass feet as I sat down at the kitchen table.

"Nobody but my kids and my mother, they're all asleep doe," she said sitting down next to Face.

"I'ma crash on da couch, til bout five in the morning. There shouldn't be that many people on the road that early. Plus I'm tryna get home to my son and daughter I know they're worrying bout me," Young said, taking his shoes off.

"Yo yung ass got kids nigga, damn I wouldn't have thought that you look like you're sixteen," Shonta spoke.

"I'm seventeen, my oldest is four years old."

Leaving them two in the kitchen talking, I walked to Shonta's room and pulled the pistol out of my waistband and sat on her bed. Then grabbed the bag of money outta her closet.

Sitting down on the bed, I looked in the bag and pulled out the one hundred and forty thousand recounted it making sure it was still there. After counting fourteen, ten thousand dollar stacks I was satisfied that everything was cool and put the money back in the bag. Going over to her dresser I pulled open the middle drawer, where I left the twenty-eight bands and made sure it was all there.

Remembering about the two hundred Vicky asked me for, I tell myself I'ma just give her a band whenever I go home.

Getting my cell phone out of my pocket I check to see if I got a reply back yet from her.

'What the fuck, she ain't hit me back? What the hell is she doing?' These are the questions that shoots thru my mind.

Hearing someone turning the doorknob and entering the room I looked up.

"Hey bae reach over there and hand me my purse, so I can give yo friend some more of them pills," Shonta says to me, seeing me with my phone in my hand.

Handing her the purse I said, "When you come back bring me something to drink."

"What do you want boo?"

"It don't really matter," I say putting the phone down on the bed next to the stacks of money.

"So what do you want a soda, or water?" Shonta asks noticing my phone light up from a text alert.

"Water would be cool," I said lying back putting my hands behind my head, feeling good with myself about all the money I just inherited after only being home a few days.

"Get ya phone one of ya hos is messaging you," she says, then walks out the door.

Opening the text, 'Fuck you ho ass nigga, why the fuck are you texting me bitch? You ain't answering yo phone cause yo around one of them stinking ass bitches you're messing wit.'

I instantly reply back this muthafucka's got life fucked up.

'Naw ho I've been out there getting this money I had this bread for you, but fuck it I'ma just give it to one of my stinking bitches I'm messing wit instead den,' I typed and hit the send button.

"Here bae," Shonta walks in with the glass of water as I sent the text.

"Thanks ma, I needed dis drink bad as fuck. My mouth was dry as hell."

Getting on the bed beside me, she said, "Who was that texting you, yo bitch?"

"Yup but, fa real doe ma, why are you worried bout who's hitting my line?"

"Cause you're over here at my shit fucking me got yo home boy on my damn couch sleeping on my shit. And on top of that whateva da hell y'all got into earlier you brought it to my house when you brought yo ass over here nigga!!"

Taking a gulp of the water her ass just gave me I sat the cup down on the night stand beside the bed.

"You wanna know something shawty you're right, everything you just said you're absolutely right but don't get this shit fucked up. I'm over here cause I'm rocking wit you, a nigga's feeling you but dat tone in yo voice you can check dat shit before I do!"

"Why are you getting mad, you asked me a question and I answered it," Shonta said, moving closer to me and placing her right leg over mine. As she threw her arm over me and rested her head on my chest.

"Naw it was yo tone of voice, I ain't mad at you bout what you said. Hell I told you that you were right. It's just not how you talk to a man, see a fuck boy is gone let you get away wit that slick shit not me."

Lifting her head up she asked, "What do you mean by slick shit?"

"Nothing bae, come here," I said, pulling her on top of me and kissing her soft lips while moving my fingers through her hair.

Before I knew it things had led from us French-kissing to us stripping one another's clothes off and, Shonta riding my dick cowgirl style as I gripped her hips.

"OHHHH OHH! Fuck yes Face! SHHHIITTT! You feel so good baby," Shonta tells me loving the feeling of my dick being in her pussy.

"I'm bout to bust in dis pussy ma."

"Noooo don't daddy let me cum first on dis dick."

"Ride dis muthafucka den ma, yo pussy is wet as fuck. Damn baby take dis dick," I said pulling her hair laying her back while still on top of me.

"OHHH SHIT! I'm finna cum on dat dick Face. Don't stop baby keep going, fuck me."

"Go ahead ma cum all over this muthafucka bae, take all this dick ma."

"Damn daddy I'm cumming, FUCKKK! You feel sooooo good OHHH!"

In one smooth motion I use my body weight and roll us over with my shaft still inside her juice box. So now she's on her stomach and I'm stroking her from the back.

"Oh shit damn nigga you're deep, I can feel you in my stomach," she says.

"Ummm hum, you feel daddy's dick bae?"

"Yesss baby damn you're killing my shit."

"Sit up on yo knees ma, let me have this pussy."

"Okay bae, fuck don't stop fucking me. Damn I'm bout to cum again."

"Arch yo back, baby and bite down on the pillow." Pounding away on her as I stuck my finger in her ass, I noticed we had been fucking on the twenty-eight thousand and the pistol she had given me.

Thinking of that Lil Wayne song, 'Pussy, Money, Weed,' I kept fucking her til we both busted our nuts. And was out of breath.

"Why did you just fuck me like dat nigga? You gone make me crazy doing shit like dat."

"How's dat gone make you crazy, I ain't do shit but put dis daddy long stroke on you."

"Aight I'm telling you keep fucking me like dat if you want to, and when I start whupping on you and yo hos. Don't ask me why I'm acting like dat."

"Chill shawty you'll be aight," I said getting up to go piss. Grabbing my phone as I walked out.

'Ho ass nigga fuck you and don't come looking for me when you can't find me!' the text from Vicky read.

Peeping that I didn't have any missed calls from her I just blew the shit off like it was one of our typical arguments. But reading the clock on my screen seeing it was 3:42 a.m. I had to call her phone.

'Damn I've been tripping over here messing with this bitch,' I thought as the phone rung in my ear.

"Hello baby what's up? Vicky!" Looking at the phone I could have sworn I just heard her pick up, now the muthafucking phone is beeping busy ...

Beep ... Beep ... Beep ... Beep ...

Hanging up I call back, pressing the redial button.

'Did she just pick up and hang up on me?' I question myself.

Beep ... Beep ... Beep ...

Getting the same results I ended the call. "Fuck man I know her ass is probably thinking I'm on some bullshit," I whispered to myself. 'But then again she might be doing her,' I thought washing my hands and leaving the bathroom.

CHAPTER 32

"Aye bruh drive safely man you know dis rental is hot as fuck too my nigga so keep yo eyes on da road bruh."

"I'm good Face trust me homie I stay on da highway fucking wit da homies, there ain't no telling what type of shit I den transported for Bang," Young stated.

"Hit me up every few hours and let me know you're good my nigga real talk."

"I got you big bruh."

Looking at the bag of money on the back seat I said, "Aight one love homie," and shut the passenger door.

"Yup one love bruh-bruh," was all I heard as the door closed. Watching him back out of the driveway I knew I would miss da lil homie. I just hoped that he made it to his destination okay.

Sliding my cell phone outta my pocket I peeped that I didn't have any messages from Victoria, but I did have a few notifications from my page on Facebook. Knowing I would check on 'em later I dialed Bang's number.

After the fifth ring he answered.

"Yoooo what's up?" Bang picked up, sounding like his throat was dry from being asleep.

"You asleep my nigga?"

"Yea who is dis Face?"

"Yea bruh, Young is on his way to you now. He just pulled out of the driveway," I informed Bang.

"Word what time is it bruh?"

"It's 5:30 a.m. my nigga he should be touching down where you are about 3:00 p.m. bruh."

"Aight bruh good looking, I'ma get at you as soon as I wake up man. Shit I just went to sleep about an hour ago."

"Get at me man fa real, I'm thinking bout making a move with you on dat shit you're out dere fucking wit," I tell him letting him know I wanted some of that heroin he's been out dere getting.

"Say no more bruh I'ma hit you up as soon as I wake up," Bang says.

"It's a bet my nigga one," I said hanging up.

Grabbing at the doorknob I heard a shuffle of some sort behind me in the neighbor's yard. Looking back I could have sworn I just saw Black standing there pointing the gun he died wit yesterday in my direction.

Looking a little harder it wasn't anybody but the man that stayed next door letting his dog out to take a pee.

"Damn I'm tripping," I tell myself and step inside closing the door behind me.

"Shonta?" I said tapping her, waking her outta her sleep.

"Huh ...?" she mumbles not even opening her eyes.

"Where are yo keys to yo car bae?"

"Huh ...?"

"Where are yo keys?" As I got my stacks of cash together.

"In my purse, why what are you bout to do?" she asked.

"I'm bout to go put this money away bae, and I'm coming right back."

"Ummm huh ... Did Young leave yet?"

"Yea I just got him up a lil bit ago boo, he's gone now doe ma."

"Did he put some fresh gauze on his shoulder?"

"Hell I don't know he might have I think," I told her not really knowing for sure.

Sitting up she looks at me and, reaching for my Mild that's in the ashtray. "Give me a light boo."

"Look at you first thing you wanna wake up and do is smoke a Mild. God damn baby," I said and passed her the lighter.

"So what nigga I'm grown as hell."

"You're right, shit you smoke more den me. What the fuck!" I said getting her keys, and fixing the pistol in my pants at the waistband.

"Nigga where the fuck were you about to go in my shit?"

"I told you I'm bout to put this money up, I ain't bout to have all of it over here."

"So what are you bout to do take it to yo bitch's house?" Shonta said, getting outta her bed walking out of the room.

"It doesn't matter where I'm bout to take my shit to I'm not bout to have it all over here," I was saying as I walked out of the room behind her.

"Face you're not bout to be playing me, coming over here fucking me, eating my pussy, sleeping, and eating my shit then going home to that bitch."

"Shonta come on with that bullshit it's too early boo. Let me hit that Black-n-Mild doe?"

"I'm telling you now man get yo shit together nigga before this shit gets deep and you get caught up," she says, as she passes the Mild.

"I got dis you just don't start acting like a madwoman and we're going to be aight ma."

"Whateva you better not be playing wit me that's all I'ma say to yo ass."

"Yea aight baby I'm gone come lock dis door," I said smacking her on the ass.

"Ouch boy stop playing! And you're just gone take the rest of the Mild?" she said following behind me.

"Here take this one bae," I gave her one that was unfreaked from outta the pack in my pocket.

"No I want dat one, dis one ain't even freaked."

"Freak it den bae."

"Ssssmuck." She smacks her lips.

I just kissed her and walked out saying, "Lock dis door I'll be back bae."

"Ooooh you get on my nerves!" she said then shut the door.

Starting the car, I'm sitting letting it heat up before I pull out. I'm looking for a CD to put on, and I hear a tap at the window. Damn near jumping outta my seat at the thought about dat muthafucka Black being the one at the window, I open the door.

"What the hell are you jumping for bae, yo scary ass?" Shonta says.

"Shit I ain't know who da hell you were wit dat damn hoodie on, what the hell do you want doe?"

"Yo phone muthafucka you forgot it, huh take it it's cold as shit out here boy," she tosses the phone on my lap and heads back inside.

"Dat's just what yo ass gets coming out here with nothing on but dat damn hoodie."

"Shut up and just hurry up and bring your ass back," she yells shutting the door.

Finding some underground 'Chief Keef,' I put the mix tape in her CD player and pulled out of her driveway.

Looking at my phone I saw that I still haven't gotten a call from Victoria. I know she's been feeling some type of way with me but damn she could at least see if I was straight out here. I hope she's home and asleep when I get there.

Zoning out on the 'Chief Keef' mix tape I wonder what life would be like growing up on the Westside of Chicago. I remember visiting before with my homeboy and his people for the Fourth of July in 2009 dat shit was straight for them few days I was there.

Turning onto my street, I wonder, 'Was Vicky's phone charged up? Or did it go dead last night when I called? Why was the busy sound coming on when I called?' Pulling into the driveway, I pulled to the back and didn't see her car ...

'Where the hell is she?' was what ran thru my mind.

Putting the car in park I hopped out and unlocked the side door with my key. 'It doesn't even look like she's been here all fucking night,' I thought.

Going to our room I put thirteen thousand dollars of the money I had on me up under the mattress. I took off the shirt I had on and put on a red Crooks T-shirt and another jacket. Cause I had given Young my jacket yesterday after that shoot out where we left Black.

Locking the house back up and getting back into the whip, I pulled out of the driveway. Making a right I see the homie Amp Jones getting outta his whip heading into his crib.

Hitting the horn he throws the deuces. And I stepped on the gas bending a few blocks.

'Is she over Kimberly's? Did she stay the night there, probably so?' I asked myself again letting my mind play tricks on me.

Before I knew it I was headed in Kimberly's direction towards the Avon Oaks. Letting myself call her phone again I waited for it to start ringing ...

Waiting I took my ear from the phone and looked at the screen. 'Did the signal go thru? It's showing that it has a connection.'

Putting the phone back to my ear, I heard what I didn't wanna hear.

Beep ... Beep ... Beep ... Beep ...

Pressing the end button I tossed the phone onto the seat next to me.

Turning onto Southern Blvd., I swore I saw her car in the parking lot of the first building where Kim lived. Straining my ears I confirmed in my mind that she was at Kim's crib, but instead of pulling over there I kept driving telling myself that she's probably just mad at me that's why she hasn't called me.

'Fuck it she'll get over it.' I tell myself.

Driving around til I'm back at Shonta's house. I pulled into the driveway, turned the car off and grabbed my phone and got out of the car. Looking at my surroundings I saw my lil bruh Five getting out of his aunt's car across the street. Knowing that I haven't heard from him in a day or two, I think like, 'What the fuck has he been up to?'

"Five what's up bruh?" yelling across the street getting his attention.

"What's good?" he says looking in my direction.

Walking to the front of the yard I throw my hand up motioning him to come here.

Seeing him fix the burner in his pants I pat mine just for procurement.

"What have you been up all night nigga?" Five questioned me.

"Naw I just followed Young to the highway making sure he ain't get pulled over by da cops, or dat none of dem fuck niggas we got into it wit at the club were out and tried some fuck shit," I lied.

"Dat nigga just went back dis morning?"

"Hell yeah dawg. Dat's a real lil nigga too man," I said thinking bout the shit we've been thru in the past ninety-six hours.

"Bruh it's definitely bout that life. What's up wit that nigga Black?" Five said.

At the mention of his name I thought, 'Should I tell him?' I told myself, 'Naw.' So I said, "He's aight still being Black."

"Dat's what's up. Aye did you see on the news that they found a dude murked in the garage over dere somewhere by Cranwood and Kenwood?"

At the moment I relived yesterday's events. Blooooud! went the .357 Smith and Wesson Black was handling like a trained killer. Next thing in one swift motion I had my burner off my waist and put six hot and readys in his ass. Blocka! Blocka! Blocka! Blocka! Blocka! Blocka! Leaving my mans stanking.

"Yo bruh what's up, you aight?" Five asked, noticing my eyes roll into the back of my head, lost in thought.

Shaking my head, bringing myself back. I said, "Yeah bruh I'm aight I'm just tired as fuck my nigga."

"Get at me in the p.m. den bro, I know you're bout to be out like a muthafucka my nigga."

"Bet dat lil bruh cause you've been on some incognito shit lately bruh."

"I'm just low right now dat's all homie. Aye doe what's up wit Strong you heard from bruh?" Five asked.

"Nope my nigga everyone's been ducked off, I wonder what the fuck is going on?"

"When you see dat nigga tell 'em to get at me bro."

"Aight," I said and embraced Five and we went our separate ways.

Looking over my shoulder I made a mental note to watch him. I could feel the thirst on him when we hugged.

CHAPTER 33

Opening my eyes, I see Shonta rolling a blunt. Getting the sleep out of my eyes I rolled over and sat up on the edge of the bed.

"Baby what time is it?" I asked.

"12:52 p.m. You were sleeping good boo, slobber was running outta ya mouth snoring and shit," she said then kissed me before lighting her spliff.

"I was dreaming my ass off too," wiping my mouth after hearing her tell me I'd been slobbering.

Getting up she closed the bedroom door to drown out the noise her children were making.

"They're bad asses are too dang loud," she said, as she dropped back onto the bed passing me the blunt.

Taking a puff, I said, "Dis is some fire who did you get this from?"

"Shay brought it with her when she came over this morning."

Lying her head on my lap I thought about getting some head from her, but then I was like, 'Naw.' Cause I gotta get up and get my day started.

"Huh take this, let me up so I can get myself together I've been sleeping too damn long as it is."

"Hold up finish smoking with me before you leave bae."

"I ain't going nowhere yet ma, I'm just putting my pants and shirt back on." Reaching into my pockets, "Where da hell is my phone?"

"It was on the floor this morning ringing, so I put it on the dresser when I got up," Shonta tells me.

"Why didn't you wake me up?" seeing my cell phone sitting next to hers on the dresser.

"Cause it probably wasn't nobody but one of yo bitches, blowing you up. I started to answer the muthafucka fa real."

Hoping it was Vicky calling me back, I picked the phone up and put in my passcode to unlock the screen. The phone showed I had eleven missed calls and three text messages.

Checking the texts first I saw that there was two from my Aunt Wiggy. She was telling me to wake up and call Rayn. They've been trying to get in touch with me.

"Here get the blunt wit your disrespectful self. Over there texting one of yo hos back!" not knowing it was my aunt.

Looking up I grabbed the blunt. "Dis is my people, ugly shut the hell up talking crazy. You don't even know what you're talking bout!"

"Whatever nigga, I told you how I am yesterday so get dem bitches in check," Shonta says, then walks out of the room to go check on the kids.

Seeing the missed calls, I see a few were from my aunt's number and also my nigga Five. But none were from Vicky. She's gotta be mad if she ain't called back, fuck it doe I'm out of here.

Calling my aunt's number, she picked up.

"Hello?" she answered.

"What's up wit you and Rayn?" I said into the phone.

"Nothing he wanted you boy, he just left for work though not too long ago. I think he's got some more of that stuff y'all be messing with."

"Where are you home?" I questioned.

"Yup, mommy just came and got da kids. So I'm by myself now. Ms. Regina just called she wants me to come over and smoke wit her."

"Shidd Aunt Wiggy come get me from da Westside," I was saying as I passed the blunt to Shonta who just walked back into da room.

"Where are you dude?" Wiggy asked.

"I'm over here in the Heights, down the street from my mom's."

"Aight well be ready I'm on my way," she told me then hung up.

"Where are you bout to go Face?" Shonta says, putting the blunt out.

"Chill wit my aunt for a min, and get to dis money. Why what's up?"

"Nothin' I was just asking, but you need to be careful out there man all this shit that is going on out there. The news was just talking about how some dude that hasn't been identified was found dead on Kenwood by multiple gunshot wounds."

Knowing what she's saying already I just stared at her, probably cause I'm high off the kush.

"Baby I hope you and your friend ain't have nothing to do with that boy getting killed."

"Man I don't know what they, you, and whoever is even talking about." Even though I know I'm the reason Black is dead. But I hoped she couldn't read me and see that I'm lying.

Looking at Face, she thinks, 'I don't believe the shit he just said to me. But who am I to judge whatever happened happened.'

"Well whatever happens bae, I just don't want yo name in it, and even though I might be trippin' ... Matter of fact just let me stop."

"Shonta what's up wit you ma? Damn like I mean you gone feel how you feel but it's either you are riding wit me or you ain't bae."

"Face I just don't wanna see you back in jail, let alone getting hurt."

"I feel you baby girl," I told her then, hugged her and kissed her forehead.

"When you leave out that door I want you to come back home to me boo," she tells me with a look of sadness on her face.

"Quit worrying yoself ma, I'm good." Hearing my phone ring I grabbed it, and answered.

"On my way out now, just keep coming down the street you'll see me Aunt Wiggy."

"Aight I'm coming down yo mom's street now."

"Aight bet," and I hung up.

Getting all my stuff, and making sure I had my money in my pockets, and my pistol I got from Shonta I was gone and out da door.

177

I heard Shonta say, "No bye, see you later, kiss or nothing nigga? Huh?"

"My bad boo." Turning around I kiss her sweet lips and said, "I'ma see you in a lil bit, aight?"

"Umm hum, be careful. And call me," she said.

Throwing my hands up to flag my aunt down she stops and lets me in her truck.

"I almost drove right past yo ass, I didn't even know that was you," Wiggy tells me as I shut the door.

"You were getting it, shidd I swore you were gon keep going too."

"Whose house are you coming from boy?" she says, ignoring what I had just said.

"This bitch's crib I've been chilling wit for a couple of days."

"I bet Vicky's been blowing you'd blow too, huh? You know you're wrong for doing that girl the way you do. Y'all been together since you were what sixteen or seventeen?"

"Yeah something like dat. But what do you mean I'm wrong for doing her the way I do? Trust me she does her little stuff too, nobody pays attention to that tho. Huh?"

"Y'all crazy if you ask me," my aunt said. "Boy all I'ma tell you is two wrongs don't make a right."

"You wanna know something tho?" I said, leaning the seat back a little, as Wiggy made a right turning onto Sixth Street heading toward Tod Ave.

"What?" Wiggy said, ashing the cigarette she was smoking.

"She hasn't called me all night or today. Her phone was ringing the first time I called last night, and I know I heard her pick up it sounded like music was playing or she was around a bunch of people. Then the phone disconnected."

"You didn't try calling back?"

"I did, I called all night but it just kept giving me the busy tone. Beep ... Beep ... Beep ... So when she didn't try getting back to me, I just took it like she was upset with me or something. Because I know for a fact she knows that was me calling."

"She was probably mad with you, shit you just got out back into the streets. And you're out here messing with these nasty bitches."

"So what now you're taking her side?" I asked taking my phone from my pocket to get on my Facebook page and check my notifications.

"When you're wrong I'ma tell you just like when you're right. But in this matter you're wrong. If I was Vicky I wouldn't have called back either."

"Yea whateva, dat's crazy," I said not looking up from my phone, cause I was keyed in on the pictures that had been posted on Victoria's page last night at some club.

'Who the fuck were them dudes in the pictures?' I thought to myself.

"See look at this shit Aunt Wiggy dis is why she ain't called me back right here. She had to take these yesterday night."

Leaning a little in her seat, after parking in Ms. Regina's driveway my aunt says, "Now she knows she ain't right for doing that. But that outfit is cute though."

"Fuck that outfit dat shit just blows the fuck outta me." Logging off my page to dial Vicky's number.

"Come on let's go smoke, before I gotta leave to go pick up my babies."

Beep ... Beep ... Beep ... Beep ... "Fuck that shit still has the busy dial tone popping up when I call."

"Try it from my phone right quick."

Grabbing my aunt's phone as she knocks on Vicky's mother's front door I dial her number.

"It's doing the same thing wit yo phone too," I said as Ms. Regina let us in.

"Hi Wiggy ... What's up Face?" Ms. Regina says. "I didn't know you were coming with her."

"She just picked me up from my mom's house, and told me we were coming over here to smoke with you right quick," I lied, but I couldn't tell her I just got scooped up from another girl's crib.

"Oh okay, where's Vicky?" she asked looking at Wiggy rolling up.

"I don't know, I was just bout to ask you if you've heard from her?"

"Nope she hasn't called me since yesterday around two in the afternoon."

"I haven't heard from her either," I say, thinking bout the pictures I just saw.

Grabbing the spliff from my aunt Ms. Regina asked me, "When was the last time you talked to her?"

"I called last night, and I know I heard someone answer the phone, but then it hung up. When I called back it was ringing busy. Her line was coming thru busy the whole night, it still is right now too."

"She didn't try calling you back?" she asked then hit the blunt and passed it to Wiggy.

"Naw, but earlier that day she texted me."

"That girl is gone call him she's just messing with his head for coming home, and getting out doing that same dumb stuff that got him locked up. Ain't no telling what else he's been doing too."

"Aunt Wiggy come on wit that B.S., you don't gotta try to put me on the spot doe," I turned my head looking wit a confused expression on my face wondering why she was tryna blow my cover.

"It's crazy she hasn't called you or nothing, cause you know how she is over you. She's definitely gone be blowing you up tryna see where you are, or what you're doing," Ms. Regina tells me.

"I already, but aye doe Ms. Regina have you heard from Rayshawn?"

"Yeah the other day he told me he was in Cleveland trying to stay out of the way."

Pulling her shirt down in the back, as she got up to walk to the kitchen, "Y'all want something to drink?"

"Yeah, here I come," my Aunt Wiggy was getting up to go to the kitchen.

"Get me something too Aunt Wiggy," I said hitting the roach on the blunt.

"Y'all wanna hit dis again before I put it out?" Hearing them both say they were cool I put the roach in the ashtray and let it burn out.

After finishing our drinks we said our goodbyes to Ms. Regina.

"Y'all be careful out dere, drive safely in this weather too Wiggy," Ms. Regina yelled from her front door as we were getting into my aunt's truck.

"Let me know if you hear from Vicky, tell her I said call me ASAP."

"I will and if you hear from her tell her butt to call me too."

"Aight I got you talk to you later," I was saying while shutting the passenger door.

Honking the horn we bugged out of the driveway.

CHAPTER 34

"I'ma hit you up later on, I might come and chill wit you and Rayn tonight."

"Aight nephew, be careful out dere boy," my aunt said as I emerged from her truck to hit the block for a min.

"I will, love you and if Vicky calls you tell her I said to get at me and quit messing around wit me."

"Love you too. I got you but you need to do right by that girl."

"What do you mean? I ain't done nothing I came home every night since I've been out except for last night."

"You know what I mean dude, and know there's always consequences for your actions too."

"I hear you I'ma get at you later auntie."

"Be safe," was all I heard after dat cause I closed the passenger door and watched her pull away.

Posted up on the side of the store that's on the corner, I was alone hopin' I could come across a nice lick or something. Before realizing I'm out here wit no dope just my pistol.

Looking over at Strong's house a few cribs down the street, I saw a lil activity. 'That nigga is getting to dat money,' I thought to myself. Then I headed inside the store.

"What's up muthafucker?" my man that runs the store said to me. This Arabic muthafucka looks just like the dude who owns the 'Holy Moley Donut Shop' off of 'Next Friday' the movie.

"What's up man? Let me get a pack of Black-n-Milds and seven of them scratch-off lottery tickets."

"How long are you gon be out this time before they get you again?" Holy Moley, asked.

"Come on man wit the bullshit bruh," I say to his ass, looking at the dude who just came into the store.

"What bullshit you're always fucking up my man. And don't be hanging out in front of my store muthafucker."

"Ring my order up so I can get the hell outta here. And where the hell are my lottery tickets bruh?"

"They're right here bruh! What damn kind do you want bruh?" this muthafucka said, snaking his neck like a broad.

"Lucky Number Sevens my nigga come on man!"

Paying for the shit I walk outside and freak one of the Milds, putting the lottery tickets in my pocket.

"Aye you, are you doing anything?" I hear someone say outta the window of a gold Chrysler Intrepid.

Looking suspiciously at the driver, I walk up tryna see who the hell is in the car with the person.

"What's up what are you tryna do?" I said to the female that's doing the talking.

She looks at the person in the back seat and turns to me and said, "I got eighty, I need something bad man."

Damn I ain't got no more work. "Let me get in wit y'all I got you."

"Come on," she says unlatching the back door behind her.

There's two bitches and a guy in the back when I get in. "Pull out and ride down the street. Where's da money"

"What are you gon give us first," the other chick says looking up at me.

"It's gon be right ma, trust me. I don't do no bullshitting."

"How do we know, you ain't even the person we came to see."

"Fuck who y'all came to see I got it."

After going thru it with them I finally talked 'em out of the eighty dollars.

"Aight turn back around and go back to the store."

"Wow dude where's the shit?" the male in the back finally speaks as I'm bout to get out of the car.

"Y'all chill right quick I got y'all, what y'all looking for dat girl, right?" I said.

"No dat food, tell me you got it man," the driver chanted.

"I got y'all, hold tight."

"Where are you going dude?" the male spoke again.

"Nowhere I got you man sit tight," I said shutting the door, jogging towards Strong's crib.

Knocking on bruh's door, he opens it and says, "What's up nigga? I was thinking you were my fein I've been waiting on."

Stepping inside outta da cold. "Aye bruh have you got some food my nigga?" I ask.

"Like what? I'm kinda low right now. I was just bout to see if you can hit yo people up and see if they're good."

"We can see my nigga, but now I'm tryna get double up on dis fifty. I got some bops at the store waiting on me." Pulling out da fifty bucks outta da eighty dey had just given me I hand it to Strong.

"I got you, let me see what I can do." Coming outta his kitchen Strong gives me eleven tickets. "Here bruh."

"I'ma be right back my nigga."

A minute or so later. "Aight be cool and hit me up I got it."

"What do you go by so I can save yo name wit da number?" the driver said.

"Just call me Face baby."

"I go by Jen, so when I call you I'ma say, 'This is Jen.' Aight?"

"Bet," I said and walked away back to Strong's spot.

"This had better be some good stuff too, or I'ma call you and be upset."

"I sure hope it is," one of the other feins said.

"Just get at me," I turned around and said, as they sped down the street.

Now chilling in Strong's crib I'm sitting there watching him boom like a muthafucka ... I just knew I had to get my hands on some of that shit.

"Bro, what's up you ain't called yo people for me?" Strong asked, sitting down passing me the blunt he just lit.

"Yeah he's talking bout give him an hour."

"Aight, bet dat."

"I got another dude who's got it too doe, right up da street but I don't know if it's fire like the stuff you just had."

"If you don't know what it's like den ain't no need fucking wit it."

"I feel it, but the nigga was talking bout seventy-five a gram doe."

"Hit 'em up, we can see what's good wit da shit. Just get a few grams just to see what da shit is hitting on. You feel me?"

"Aight, I'm finna see what's up wit some of it too my nigga. It seems like dat's where da money is."

"It's definitely where da bread is bruh."

"I can tell, you've been booming in dis bitch," I replied passing the blunt back.

"Oh yeah bruh I saw Five dis morning, right? He was talking bout when I see you tell you to holla at him."

Quizzically Strong stared at me. "What did he want? Shidd dat nigga definitely knows where we stand. You dig my nigga?"

"Dat shit is crazy my nigga, but you know it was them tho or you just feel like dat?"

Hitting the loud then passing it back before coughing ... "I know it was him and dat nigga he be wit bruh."

I just hit the loud. Picked up my phone and tried hitting my mans up from 'Claney's' my cuz A.D. turned me on to.

"Speak up," was how he answered the phone.

"What's poppin' my nigga, are you good?"

"Always, who is dis doe?"

"Face mob, bruh what's good are you around da way?"

Seeing Strong get up and come back with the chrome Sig nine millimeter, I wondered what the hell he was on. But whatever it is it must be some bullshit.

"Aight my nigga give me a minute I'll be dere," I said and ended the call.

"Yo what's that nigga's number?" Strong asked, as he sat the hammer on the table in front of himself.

"Who bruh?"

"Dat ho ass nigga Five?"

"It's in here somewhere bruh, let me look thru my contact list."

"Dese niggas out here think it's a game Face. I'ma show 'em doe, him and dat nigga Junie. I've been waiting for 'em to show their faces around here dawg I'ma light dey asses up," Strong expressed himself standing up and tucking the Sig in the waistband of the jeans he wore.

"The number is ... 766-6518, look man just see what bruh is on before you start flexing my nigga."

Grabbing the cell on the table. "Dat's 330 right?"

"Yup," I answered and thought, 'Why da fuck did I just let the nigga call Five? But fuck it that's what the nigga said he wanted me to do.'

I'm zoned out in my thoughts, but I'm hearing Strong and Five in a heated conversation. Pacing from the back room to the kitchen I see Strong's facial expression and can tell he wants war with Five.

"I'ma see you ho ass nigga, I know dat was y'all!" ... Strong pauses like he's listening to whatever it is Five's saying.

"Yeah whatever nigga it's on!" Strong says before hanging up on Five.

"So what's up?" I asked, passing the blunt.

"What do you mean? Bruh I know dem fuck niggas got me and I'ma see bout dem niggas," Strong says, irritated but tryna stay sane.

"Are you still trying to see what's good with the dope from ol' boy I just holla'ed at?"

"Yeah let's ride. But dese niggas think it's a game doe man," he said tucking his burner in his waistband.

I wasn't gonna ask but, I couldn't resist the urge I felt to know what was said. So I did what anybody else would do and I said, "What was dat nigga talking bout bruh?"

"Nothing tryna deny the shit like I just jumped off the porch or some shit."

"Word! My nigga let me get at him before you get in too deep and I have to attend one of y'all's funerals bruh."

"On my momma! Face, bruh ah dead man walking."

Shaking my head I look at Strong and can see he means every word he just said.

"Come on man let's go see what dis work is looking like, you need to get that off yo mind. And get back to the money my nigga."

"Hold up let me go grab a few bands from upstairs, cause if this shit is official I'ma cop a sleeve so I ain't gotta bullshit wit these other niggas."

Damn bruh is talking bout a sleeve, dat's nine ounces and dat's about fourteen thousand, five hundred dollars if da homie ain't taxing. Yeah dis nigga Strong is eating off dis heroin shit, I gotta get on and quit bullshitting. A nigga might as well get it while it's good.

"Yo are you ready bruh?" Strong says breaking my train of thought.

"Fa sho my nigga. But what's up with the bag?" I said seeing the Jordan gym bag.

"Dis is thirty-five thousand dollars right here bruh, if da nigga ain't taxing I'ma go ahead and get a half a brick and two and a quarter."

'Damn dis bitch is eating,' I think, getting up to leave out the door with Strong.

CHAPTER 35

"I ain't gon front bruh, I ain't know you were eating like dis homes." Bobbing my head to the low beat playing in the background as Strong and I chop it up.

"I'm on another level with this hustling, my nigga dat's why muthafuckas are at a nigga man. See you got hustlers, robbers, lazy muthafuckas, and hard-working people who push da clock for a living."

"No doubt bruh, I can see dat."

"I had to buckle down and get serious to get where I am, and I'll be damned if I watch a nigga take something from me I worked hard for. Dat's why I gotta make an example outta dem niggas who tried me. Dey got at me but dey missed, but trust me I ain't gone miss I'm bout to hit 'em hard."

"I hear you bruh but just focus on dis bread, I'm tryna eat wit you," I said being serious, but at the same time tryna get him from thinking bout that other shit.

"I got you bruh," Strong says, as he's turning into Claney's parking lot.

"Aight bet, but just know that I ain't tryna get in the middle of you and Five's beef."

Parking and turning the engine off, he looks at me and said, "You got dat bruh. Call dat nigga and tell 'em we're out here."

Searching thru my cell log in my phone I found the number I was looking for and pressed the call button.

After the fourth ring he answered ... "What's up?"

"I'm outside," I replied.

After being there bullshitting around with da plug, Strong and I leave with a half a key and two and a half ounces for Strong. And a four-way for myself, I end up coming outta seventy-two hundred dollars. But just seeing how the feins fuck with my nigga heavily I know this was the right lane for me.

"Y'all be careful driving with that shit dawg. Trust me that's a life sentence if y'all get caught slippin' fucking around," Worm says, with a blunt hangin' out of his mouth.

"Nigga's bout to go and tuck dis shit my nigga but good looking doe."

"Face you might as well come back to my spot right quick so I can get dis work off of me then I'll shoot you wherever you're tryna go," Strong said hitting the horn and chucking the deuce to Worm, as we pulled outta the parking lot.

Saluting Worm I turned to Strong and told him, "I'm with you my nigga, I ain't trippin' I'm tryna get to dis money."

"Say no more bruh, I'm bout to introduce you to a whole other world."

"Where the fuck is Vicky?" I questioned, myself thinking I would just take the heroin I just got to the crib. But with her missing in action like she's been I quickly erased that thought outta my mind.

"Bruh grab that bag off of the back seat, I gotta take a piss right quick. It feels like I'm bout to pee all over myself," Strong says, turning off the engine and hopping out rushing into the house to take a leak.

Grabbing the bag that was just full of money, but now contains twenty-four and a quarter ounces of dope. I stepped out of the car after locking the doors, and walked into Strong's back door into the kitchen and locked the door behind me.

Setting the bag down on the counter I think about all the money I'm bout to make. Not believing I just stepped into the big leagues.

'I'm getting money still getting money / Catch me in the trap wit dem fifties and dem hunnids /,' was the ringtone my phone was playing taking me outta my thoughts. 'Who the hell is this?' I think as I reach into my pocket to get the phone out.

Seeing it was a number I didn't recognize I sent the caller to voicemail. 'I don't know who the fuck that was,' I say to myself setting the phone on the countertop.

"Aye bruh you know what you're doing with this shit man?" Strong asked me, coming into the kitchen reaching into the Jordan bag pulling nothin' but ether out.

"Got damn that shit is strong as a bitch," I said as Strong opened the half a key up.

"Aye reach into that drawer in front of you and get dem face masks out."

Handing him the mask he says, "Nigga you still ain't answered my question."

"What's dat bruh?" I said putting the mask over my mouth and nose.

"My nigga do you know what you're doing fucking with dis shit?"

"Fa sho bruh, what do you think this is my first time around dis shit?" I lied, but I couldn't let lil bruh know that this was my first time busting heroin down and packing it up.

"We're definitely bout to find out, my blender is in that cabinet grab it for me bruh."

"Here bro," I said passing him the blender.

'I'm getting money still getting dat money / Catch me in the trap wit them fifties and dem hunnids /.' Hearing my phone ringing again I see it's the same number I just sent to my voicemail. I waited a few seconds before I answered the call. Before speaking I just sat there tryna detect who it was calling.

After making it out in my mind it was a female's voice that just said, "Hello?" I said, "Hello, who is dis?" thinking it was Vicky finally getting at me after a few days of being upset.

"Oh you don't know my voice?" she says.

"Shidd ma I ain't even know, whose number this is that you're calling from. But now hearing your voice I know who you are."

"Why haven't I heard from you in a few days Face? I've been inboxing you on your page and texting you and you've just been on some fuck me shit."

"Nikki chill out baby girl it ain't like dat I've just been tryna get to this money. You feel me?"

"I understand but damn you can get at me, and see what I want Face."

Looking at Strong drop chunks of the dope in the blender with some powdered substance to cut it wit. Being unfamiliar with the powdered substance I zoned baby girl out and asked Strong, "Aye bro what's that shit you're mixing wit the dope?"

"Huh?" Strong says, turning his attention towards me, so he can understand what I'm saying.

"What's dat shit bro?" I ask, still wit the phone to my ear.

"Dis is methadone I use it to cut the dope with. It's like a synthetic addictive narcotic that's used as a substitute for heroin."

"Fa sho bruh, I ain't even know dat my nigga," I tell 'em, taking a mental note to remember what to use to cut the food wit.

"Hello boy got damn I know you didn't forget you were on the phone," Nikki says sounding as if she's built herself up an attitude.

"Naw shawty I ain't forget, but let me call you back in a minute I'm tryna handle something."

"Oh my God, you're so rude."

"How's dat rude? All I said is let me call you back."

"I got something important I needed to talk to you bout so you better call me back Face."

"I got you baby girl. Just give me a hot minute to take care of what I'm doing."

"Bye dude," she says hanging up in my ear.

'Man I gotta get my shit together wit dese women,' I thought as I put the cell phone in my pocket.

"You still got dem hos on yo team I see nigga," Strong says, turning off the blender and removing the lid.

"You know how I do baby boy, dis shit don't stop. I need to get myself together doe, I ain't heard from wifey all day. Shit really not since the other day."

"Who Vicky?"

"Man you already know dat's wifey bruh. Ain't no question. Ya dig?"

"Naw my nigga ain't no telling wit yo ass."

"Get the fuck outta here wit dat shit dawg ain't none of these hos before my bitch."

"Yeah right," he replied but by the way he said it I can tell he didn't believe a word I just said.

"Serious business bruh, but I will say dis broad I've been fucking on got some fire, I ain't been to the crib or nothing. Vicky ain't answering her phone for me or called no nothing my nigga."

"Fuck it bruh get to dis money," he tells me, as he mixes more dope inside the mixer with the methadone substitute.

"No doubt bruh dat's mandatory," I said while pulling out the seventy-eight hundred dollars I had in my pocket and started counting it.

There's something bout da way money makes you feel when you're counting it that I just love.

"Aye, you want me to cut your work up for you?" asking me as he put the top on the blender cutting it on.

"Yeah bro just bust down like two and a half of it for me for now."

"You sure bruh?"

"Yup," I said, while dialing Nikki's number calling her back like I said I would.

CHAPTER 36

"Damn dawg dat's crazy, shorty tryna put a baby on you like dat," Strong says, stopping for the red light.

"Fa real doe she had brought it up to me before in 2009. But when I told her bout us getting a blood test she said aight, but then turned around and bounced out to California somewhere."

"Ain't no way shawty could have been serious bout that situation if she did dat."

"Same shit I was thinking, on some real shit, I had started thinking da ho really tried me like dat after she'd seen me in dat Delta 88 I had on dem 22's."

"I ain't gone say dat, cause knowing you yo ass wasn't wearing no condom my nigga."

"You're right but, we weren't in a committed relationship den either. So for a fact I know she was getting dick from somewhere else besides me."

Going thru the intersection as the light turned green. Strong peeps the cop car to his right.

"Dere go the boys bruh be careful homie."

"I see 'em."

'I'm dirty as fuck,' I say to myself as I'm looking in the passenger side mirror.

"Fuck dey made a right behind us."

"Don't panic bruh just drive smoothly," I tell him but really my heart is beating like it's bout to jump outta my chest.

"We're going to yo house right?" he asked making a right onto my street.

"Hell yeah shit it's da closest, fuck driving to Shonta's crib."

"Damn he turned behind us again man."

"Chill bruh yo plates and stuff are up to date right?"

"Yeah man. Which house is it, dis white one on da left?" he asked hitting the left blinker.

"Yeah bruh." 'God please don't let 'em hit the lights on us,' I prayed to myself. Pulling into the driveway safely I thanked the Lord for answering my prayer.

"Damn homie I think that might have been Webber's bitch ass too dawg."

"Dey was on dis muthafucka too, looking as a bitch bruh."

"Let's go in for a min, cause I ain't tryna leave just yet. I know for a fact he's gon pull us over."

"Come on my nigga," I said getting out of da car.

Unlocking the house door we stepped inside.

"Make yoself at home my nigga. Roll up, there's something to drink in the refrigerator," I told Strong as I made my way to the back to put the dope and the seven thousand up with the other thirteen thousand I got put up leaving myself with eight hundred left in my pocket.

'Damn I could have just went to prison for the long haul,' I sit on my bed and think once I had put the bread and dope up. Dis is crazy as hell, why hasn't Vicky's ass hit me up yet? She knows I tried to reach her, and from the looks of things she hasn't been at the house.

"Strong, you roll that shit yet my nigga?"

"Dat's what I'm doing now homie," he yells back, as I pulled out my phone and sent Vicky a text.

'Baby what's up where are you? I got that paper you asked me for the other day. I can tell you haven't been home, I hope all is well with you baby girl. Love you!'

I pressed send on the text message and got up and went in the front with Strong.

Sitting on the couch across from where Strong sat, he must have read my mind cause he said to me, "Face, where's Vicky you still ain't heard from her?"

Hunching my shoulders, and shaking my head. "She's been M.I.A. my nigga I just texted her though."

"What the hell did you do for her to go missing in action like dis dawg?"

"Nothing really we had some words bout nothing. But I guess she's on some other type."

Lighting the flame to the blunt Strong asked, "Words like what?" he says, taking a deep pull.

"Nothing my nigga, she had wanted me to shoot her some bread to take care of the water bill or whatever. The water company came over here and shut the shit off, but at the time I was fucked up and ain't have it."

"But you got it now doe?"

"Fa sho, and I've been trying to reach her and let her know dat. But she ain't put up her phone and called me back."

"There's something to dat bruh, cause knowing her like I do, she ain't gon just bounce on you like dat."

"I already know man," I said reaching for the blunt as he passed it to me.

The thought of her being with another man enters my mind as I hit the loud pack. And it's like Strong then read my mind again because he asked the same thing I was just thinking.

"You think she's with another dude or something?"

Taking a deep breath I sigh and say, "I don't know bruh. But it is what it is though."

The ringing of my cell phone has gotten my attention. It's from an area code that I'm unfamiliar with, I let it ring a few more times then I pick up.

"Yo who is dis?" I answered.

"Dis is Bang nigga what's up?"

"Ain't nothing bruh, just cooling at da crib. Why what's up fool?" I ask tryna see what this call is about.

"Shidd man, I was just thinking right? You said you're tryna get down wit me, right?"

"Fa sho, my nigga," I respond, and hand Strong the loud after taking a hit filling my lungs.

"Well you know I respect how you handled things down dere when shit got real, you ain't panicked you just went ahead and knocked dat shit off and made sure things was right. So with that being said I'ma be sending you a play on da face in a day or two. Let me put it together and I'ma get at you homie."

"I'm game my nigga just when you get ready to swing my way put me on beat so I can be prepared bruh. I might have something already ready to put on the tab."

"No doubt bruh, just pick up when I hit you."

"It's a bet my nigga. So I take it everything went good with Young?"

"Most definitely homie," Bang said letting me know the drive was safe.

"I fucks with dat little nigga man, tell him I said he's welcome anytime to come thru and fuck wit me bruh."

"Aight bruh you be safe and pick up, when it's time to bust dis move we bout to put in play."

"Fa sho bruh just hit me up homie," I told Bang ending the call.

CHAPTER 37

The next morning ...

'Damn I was knocked out like a muthafucka,' I think to myself after realizing I had fallen asleep on the couch.

Getting up tryna get my day started. Grabbing my phone off the table. I see hella missed calls and texts.

'Fuck I was gone like a muthafucka last night that loud pulled me down. Hold up when the hell did Strong leave?' I say to myself as I dial his number. 'Dis bitch still ain't brought her ass home or called up a nigga,' I think as I wait for Strong to pick up.

Letting the line ring several times I end the call. 'He must be still asleep,' I tell myself. 'What time is it anyway?' I think, as I look at my screen saver for the first time.

7:38 a.m., man I had to go to sleep early last night for me to be up this early.

Who the fuck are all these missed calls and shit from?

Nikki, Shonta, private, private, private, and Nikki again. Rayn, my cuz and some more private calls ...

That most definitely had to be one of the bitches calling private like dat.

Seeing the first text I noticed it was from Shonta. "Damn dat's how you're doing it nigga, you must be up under your bitch?"

Going to the next message it reads, 'So you ain't gone answer?'

And the following message, which I see is from Nikki says, 'Nigga you ain't anything, don't worry though a bitch ain't bout to stress over no dick. Lying ass nigga fuck you.'

'I forgot all about her ass,' I think to myself. 'Oh well,' I think and put my phone down to brush my teeth. Walking into the bathroom I got my toothbrush put some toothpaste on it, grab my washcloth and then turn on the water.

"Aww fuck," I say forgetting about the hot water.

Running my toothbrush under the cold water, I proceed to brush my teeth. "Where the hell is Victoria?" my thoughts wandered as I brush away.

"This shit is crazy how she's playing these bogus ass games." I spit the toothpaste and spit in the toilet bowl, and tried to flush it and ain't nothing happen.

Rinsing my mouth out and washing my face I walk out of the bathroom, and into the bedroom.

Sitting on my bed I think, 'What am I bout to do today I know I have to move this dope and get to the money. This mess wit Victoria is really getting to me. What type of games is she playing?'

Getting up off the bed I grab the twenty thousand outta the stash and thumb thru it. 'Man just a week ago I was locked up in the Trumbull County Jail broke as fuck,' I think as I put the money down and look for the dope I just put away last night.

Hearing my phone ring, I drop the dope with the money and jog off to the living room. 'I hope dis is Vicky's fucking ass,' I think as I reach the living room and get my phone. Looking at the screen I see it's my Aunt Wiggy.

"Hello what's up?" I said, going back to the room.

"Boy where are you?"

"I'm at the crib Aunt Wiggy what's up?"

"Rayn said you're tryna smoke?"

"Yeah come thru and scoop me up right quick, I gotta get in the shower at y'all's crib tho. Because our water got shut off."

"Aight well you can do that after we drop Rayn off at work."

"Where are y'all now?" I ask, putting the money back up where I had tucked it.

"Coming across the bridge on Summit St."

"Aight."

"We'll be pulling up in about ten minutes be ready cause you know he's gotta be at work."

"It's on, I'ma see you when y'all pull up."

"Bye," she tells me hanging up in my ear.

Tossing the cell phone on the bed I grab the work I was taking with me and put the rest up. Putting together an outfit and some underclothes, I was ready and waiting for my aunt to pull up.

Getting the chrome Sig from under the couch I placed it on the table. 'I hope I don't run into no bullshit today,' I thought as I texted Vicky's number. 'Hey baby I hope that everything is fine with you. I'm bout to leave the house, I've been here all night. I would have thought you would have called me or texted by now. You haven't even been to the house or nothing ma. Get at me ASAP, I'm leaving the money for the water bill and a few dollars for yoself in the top drawer with your panties and bra ... I love you, get at me baby girl.'

Ending the message and pressing send I heard a horn blow outside. My phone rang and seeing that it was my aunt, I answered. "I'm on my way out now."

"Boy come on you should have been ready."

"I'm coming now," I said, and pressed the end button.

Pulling five hundred dollars out of the eight hundred dollars I had in my pocket, I put it in the top drawer. Getting my outfit and underclothes I headed out the door, but not without my chrome Sig.

"What's up y'all?" I spoke as I climbed in the back seat of my aunt's Expedition.

"Nothing nigga I just wanted to holla at you before I go to work, this dude is tryna get some of that dog food," Rayn says, getting my attention.

"Word who is he doe unk?"

"Dis square type nigga dat I work wit."

"You know dis shit is crazy cause I just touched down wit some of dat shit last night for da low, not even knowing who I was gone sell dat shit to."

"You got some right now?" he said turning around looking at me.

"Here bae take dis," Wiggy says, handing Rayn da blunt of loud as she put the truck in reverse and bugged out of the driveway.

"Dis is what it's looking like right here," I tell him pulling out the packs I had on me from last night.

I handed him the bag of heroin, and let him examine it as I sat back and thought about the money I was hoping to make from the shit.

"Here neph take dis," he says, extending his arm passing the loud to me.

Hitting the kush I instantly coughed exposing my lungs to the strong grade of marijuana.

"Man this is some fire, when did you get dis?"

"That's the same shit you got from me the other day. Well it's some new shit but it's the same product."

Hitting my chest tryna help clear the smoke that I swallowed I hit the loud a few more times and passed the blunt back to the front.

"How much of this shit right here do you got doe neph?" Rayn says.

"I got a couple ounces of dat right dere."

"So what do you want for all dis?"

"Dat's a whole zip, I'll take like twenty-five hundred dollars for it like dat."

Tryna work his head unk said, "Neph are you gon tax me like dat?"

"I ain't taxing I'm just tryna get me, I gotta make something off dat shit."

"Let me call dis nigga and see what he's tryna do before I take this off yo hands."

"Bae you wanna stop and get something to eat to take to work with you?" Wiggy says, handing Rayn the kush.

"You can just stop at Wendy's since it's right there across from my job."

While he's on the phone chopping it up with whoever it was that he's talking to, I'm sitting there wondering what the hell's up with Victoria's ass.

"Aight that's what it is then bruh, I'ma see you when you come in," Rayn tells the dude. "I'm bout to pull in now my nigga, in like ten minutes. I'm grabbing something to eat and I'ma see you."

"Bae what do you want?" Wiggy asked.

"Get me a Double Jr. Bacon Cheeseburger Meal and a Chocolate Milkshake. Do you want something Face?"

"Uhh yeah, just get me the same shit," I respond reaching into my pocket to retrieve the money for the order.

After pulling away from the drive-thru we go to the parking lot of the glass shop, where Rayn worked.

"Park by that car right dere bae," Rayn says pointing his finger.

"Unk look just shoot me twenty-three hundred dollars for dat shit and you can make a quick two hundred dollars for yoself."

"Bet neph, dat's a good copy."

I wasn't sweating it cause I figured I just made a quick five hundred dollars profit off the shit and still got a few ounces put up.

Getting out of the truck unk goes and busts his move with the dude. I could see the person hand unk some bread and unk pass him the pack. He's examining the dope closely then reaches over and tucks it into the glove box and they exit the vehicle.

"If that's some fire he'll be wanting more of it ASAP, here go yo paper. Catch up with me later on man and we'll blow something."

"It's a bet, and definitely be expecting him to get at you unk," I said, grabbing the money from him.

Leaning in to give my aunt a kiss unk gets his food and turns around to walk into work.

"Love you baby," Rayn says.

"I love you too bae," Wiggy replies, then hits the horn as I climb into the front seat.

"Get at me later unk!" I yelled and slammed the door.

CHAPTER 38

Retrieving the Black-n-Mild outta my pocket I started twisting it between my fingers, freaking it so it'll smoke better to my liking.

"You wanna go to my house now so you can shower and get dressed, or are you coming wit me?" Wiggy asked.

"Yea take me to your house so I can get myself together right. Dis Wendy's smells good as hell, I ain't had none of this in a minute," referring to me just being locked up for the past few months.

Putting the Mild down, I looked into the Wendy's bag and pulled my sandwich out and took a bite.

"What's up Aunt Wiggy, what are you about to do?"

"Go to mommy's right quick, and check on her."

"Tell her I ain't forgot about her plate. I'ma bring it back."

Pulling in front of her house, she turns the truck off and hands me the keys to the house so I can open the door.

"Hurry up boy and bring my keys back so I can go."

"Aight."

Unlocking the door I turned around and see my aunt running towards me.

"Watch out dude I gotta pee," she says brushing right past me.

Going to the truck I get my stuff and bring it inside the house and finish eating my sandwich and fries.

Coming from the bathroom, Wiggy's racing down the steps.

"Where are my keys? I gotta go. And if you leave lock my door."

"They're right dere in the hallway on the stand." Remembering I left my phone in her car, I follow her out the door.

"Aunt Wiggy hand me my phone right quick," I said, standing on her side of the truck.

"Where is it boy?" she responds looking for it.

"It should be right there in front of you."

"I don't see no damn phone Face."

"Hold up Aunt Wiggy, cause I know I ain't got it," I tell her, as I walked to the passenger side of the truck.

Opening the door, the phone rings and I pick it up from between the door and the seat.

Not recognizing the number I answered, hoping it was Vicky. But what I got wasn't something that I would have expected in a million years.

"Hello, who is dis?" I asked.

"Face? Victoria's dead!" the caller yelled into my ear.

"What?! What happened to her?!"

"Her and Kimberly!" the caller screams again.

"Ms. Regina what happened?"

"I don't know, I'll call you back I gotta call dis lady and try to find out," she says and hangs up in my ear.

Looking at my aunt I said, "Victoria's dead Aunt Wiggy," then closed my eyes and let my head hit the headrest.

"Uh uh stop playing," she says.

I looked at her again and said, "I'm for real that was Ms. Regina who just called me."

"What happened?"

"I don't know she said she's gon call me back."

Grabbing her phone.

"Let me call her and see ..."

... was all I heard I was lost in deep thoughts.

'What happened to Vicky?'

'How long has she been dead?'

'Why wasn't I there for her?'

Before I knew it the truck was in motion leaving the door to the house unlocked, with us en route to see my mother-in-law.